"I'M TAKING THE BOAT OUT," MICHAEL ANNOUNCED.

Biting back a sob, Molly whispered, "But what if . . ."

The policeman cursed at the sound of the engine coming to life. "Jesus, O'Hara," he muttered as the boat began to move.

"What time is it?" Molly asked with a dawning sense of horror.

"Just before midnight. Why?"

"I don't know. Just a feeling I have."

"That the bomb would be set for midnight," Ken guessed.

She shook her head. "One minute after."

Both men regarded her with puzzlement. "Why?"

"The date," she said with certainty, her voice choked. "It'll be the anniversary of the god-damned Cuban revolution."

"Twelve-oh-one," Ken said.

Molly's eyes burned from tears and from straining to see through the darkness. There was no mistaking the sudden spark of fire at the back of the boat, the puff of smoke. "Oh, God," she murmured, wanting to turn away.

Just when she thought she could bear the terrible suspense not one second longer, flames shot into the air with an explosion of sound that slammed through the stillness and echoed in her head. . . .

Also by Sherryl Woods

A MOLLY DEWITT ROMANTIC MYSTERY

HOT
SCHEMES

SHERRYL WOODS

A DELL BOOK

Published by
Dell Publishing
a division of
Bantam Doubleday Dell Publishing Group, Inc.
1540 Broadway
New York, New York 10036

The trademark Dell® is registered in the U.S. Patent and Trademark Office.

ISBN: 0-440-21486-6

Printed in the United States of America

Published simultaneously in Canada

September 1994

10 9 8 7 6 5 4 3 2 1

RAD

Acknowledgments

A very special thanks to Isaura Pino and Susana Betancourt for speaking Spanish far better than I do and for keeping the emotions in this book honest. And to Heather Graham, Joan Johnston, Carla Neggers, Meg O'Brien, and Sally Schoeneweiss—all of whom know how to turn a phrase—for listening to me yell when my words aren't flowing exactly right. And last, but definitely not least, to Damaris Rowland—an extraordinary editor—for her unsinkable faith in Molly and Michael.

CHAPTER
ONE

The deafening music pulsed to a Latin beat at Sundays by the Bay, a favorite weekend watering hole of Miami boaters and the singles crowd. Molly DeWitt had long since given up any attempts to carry on a conversation with Detective Michael O'Hara, whose attention seemed to be focused more on the horizon than on her anyway. His beer sat untouched, warming in the sun. As near as she could tell with his eyes shaded by his favorite reflective sunglasses, he hadn't even noticed the five scantily clad women at the next table. That was how she knew he was far more worried than he was letting on.

"Still no sign of your uncle's boat?" she shouted over the music.

He glanced at her briefly, shook his head, then turned his attention back to the water. His expression was more somber than she'd ever seen it, even in the midst of some particularly gruesome homicide investigations.

Molly understood his concern. It was now after noon. Tío Miguel should have been back by eleven o'clock, noon at the latest, from his regular Sunday fishing trip. On days he took out charters, he might stay out longer, but Sundays were personal. On Sundays he stayed only long enough to catch enough snapper or grouper for the family's dinner, plus extra to share with friends up and down the block in their Little Havana neighborhood.

The rest of the week Tío Miguel worked nights delivering the morning newspaper door-to-door, then took out his occasional small fishing charters, usually wealthy Latin Americans and their Miami business associates. One or two days a week he worked on the boat, fiddling with the engine to assure top performance, polishing the trim, cleaning it from stem to stern. Though the charter boat wasn't new or top of the line, it was his most prized possession and he cared for it with passionate devotion.

A small, olive-complexioned man with a deep tan and dark-as-midnight eyes, Miguel García had an unmistakable wiry strength even though he was about to turn sixty-five. Molly had met him several months earlier at dinner at Tío Pedro's, yet another of Michael's uncles. She had been instantly charmed by his awkward, soft-spoken blending of English and Spanish and the pride in his voice as he talked of Michael's accomplishments in Miami.

Tío Miguel and Tío Pedro and their wives—both sisters of Michael's mother—had preceded Michael to Miami when Fidel Castro succeeded Batista in Cuba. They had left behind homes, family, and once-thriving careers in the hope of regaining freedom. It was to them, via one of the famed Pedro Pan airlifts, that Michael's mother had sent him, alone, at the age of five.

Though Molly had known many other exiles, some successful, some barely making it, none had touched her quite the way Tío Miguel had. When he talked of his native land, there had been such sadness in his eyes and something more, an anger perhaps, that his homeland was out of reach to him now. Unlike his brother-in-law Pedro, who owned a flourishing Cuban restaurant and whose children were now involved in careers of their own, Tío Miguel had never fully adapted to his new land.

Like so many other Cuban exiles who had come to Miami in the sixties and who had expected to go back at any moment, Tío Miguel had struggled with English. Fortunately, he lived in a community where shopkeepers spoke Spanish, where parish priests and government officials spoke his language. He had settled for taking menial jobs to support his family, always with the fragile hope that he would return home to a free Cuba someday. As time passed, hope had faded, replaced now by sorrow and the faintest traces of anger and bitterness.

Molly glanced at Michael and saw that his attention was still avidly focused on Biscayne Bay and the Atlantic beyond.

"You're worried, aren't you?" she said.

"He's never been this late before, not on Sunday when he knows Tía Pilar will be waiting and the family will be gathering after Mass."

"Does he have a radio on the boat?"

Michael nodded.

"Then he can call the Coast Guard if he's in trouble. I'm sure he's okay. He probably found a hot spot where the fish were really biting and didn't want to come in yet."

"Maybe," he said tersely. He stood up. "I'm going inside to make a call. Keep an eye out for him, will you?"

"Of course."

Though Tío Miguel had invited Michael, Molly, and her son, Brian, to come fishing with him some Sunday, they had never taken him up on it. Brian had brought it up once or twice, but Molly had discouraged him from pressing Michael about it. Now as she watched the endless rows of sailboats, yachts, and fishing boats dotting the water beyond the marina, she realized she had no idea what his boat was named, much less what it looked like. Except for those with billowing sails, they all looked pretty much alike to her, especially from this distance.

When Michael finally returned, he looked more tense than he had before.

"What did you find out?"

"Nothing. Tía Pilar said she was expecting him home by now, that he'd said nothing about being later than usual. There was something else in her voice, though, that convinced me I'm right to be worried. I called the Coast Guard. They haven't had any distress calls, but they're going out to take a look." He didn't have to say that he'd called in a favor to accomplish that. He drummed his fingers nervously on the table and took another sip of beer. "Damn, I can't stand this. Come on."

"Where?"

"I'll run you home, then come back and rent a boat. I'm going out myself. I've been fishing with him enough. I probably know better than the Coast Guard does where to start looking." He threw some money on the table, then slipped between the tightly packed tables along the edge of the marina.

They were nearly at the car when Molly touched his arm. "Michael, I want to go with you," she said, unable to ignore his anxiety. She'd learned long ago that Michael was incapable of asking for help, but that didn't mean he couldn't use a little support from a friend once in a while. Predictably, though, he was already shaking his stubborn Cuban-Irish head.

"No. If there's trouble, I don't want you involved."

"What sort of trouble?" she said, puzzled by the implication that something other than an engine breakdown might have delayed Tío Miguel.

He just shook his head again, his expression more tight-lipped and obstinate than usual. "You're going home."

Molly made up in determination what she lacked in stature. And when someone she cared about was in trouble, she didn't want to waste time debating her right to help. She planted herself in front of him, eyes blazing.

"Dammit, Michael O'Hara, don't you pull any of this Latin machismo stuff with me. Two pairs of eyes will be better than one out there. If your uncle is hurt, I might be able to help. You won't be able to manage him and the boat at the same time."

Apparently he saw that arguing would simply waste more precious time. That was the only explanation she could think of for his quick, grudging nod. He changed directions so quickly, she almost lost her footing trying to keep up with him.

Halfway down the marina's first dock, a middle-aged fisherman was just unloading his catch. He greeted Michael with a nod. *"Hola."*

Michael began talking to him in Spanish.

The only thing Molly understood for certain was Tío Miguel's name, but the man's head bobbed in agreement.

"He'll take us out," Michael told her, already following the man onto the boat. He held out his hand to help Molly aboard. "He and my uncle are friends. Tío's slip is just two down," he said, gesturing toward the empty space. "He says my uncle went out as usual about dawn."

"Does Tío Miguel usually fish in the same place?" Molly asked.

"More or less. We might have to do some cruising around though. I assume you don't get seasick. The water looks a little choppy today."

"Let's just say it's probably best if we don't put the idea into my head," she said just as the powerful engine started throbbing beneath them. Her stomach churned, then settled a bit as they eased away from the dock and into open water. Fresh air replaced gas fumes as they chugged out of the harbor. She tried to ignore the thick, dark clouds gathering in the west and the threat they represented.

"You okay?" Michael asked, removing his sunglasses to peer at her more closely. "You looked a little green there for a minute."

"I'm fine now."

"I want to get up front to help Raúl watch for the boat. You'll be okay back here?"

Molly nodded. "What's the name of the boat? I'll watch from here."

"The *Niña Pilar.*"

She reached out and touched his hand. "We'll find him, Michael."

"I hope so," he said, and turned abruptly, but not before she'd noted the tense set of his jaw and the deepening worry in his eyes in that instant before he'd slipped his sunglasses back into place.

Not only was he Tío Miguel's namesake, but the two shared a special bond because of Michael's young age when his mother had sent him to America to live with his aunts and uncles. That, combined with the fact that Michael had never known his own Irish-American father, had cemented their relationship. The closeness was not something Michael ever spoke of, but she had learned over the last months to read the emotions in his eyes, even when his words revealed nothing. If something had happened to Tío Miguel, Michael would be devastated, as would the rest of the close-knit family.

Under the blinding glare of the early-afternoon summer sun, a fine mist of salty water dried on Molly's skin almost as soon as it landed, leaving her skin gritty. As the boat chugged into deeper seas, the water turned from a glistening silver to a murky green, then purple, darkened from above by the bank of nearly black clouds rolling in, dumping sheets of rain in the distance and hiding the land from sight.

Whether it was due to the violence of the

approaching storm or Michael's anxiety, Molly grew increasingly uneasy as the boat rocked over the choppy waves. All the other boats were making for land, while they continued to head out to sea.

No longer able to stand being left alone, she made her way forward on the slippery deck, clinging to the metal railing as she climbed up to join Michael and Raúl. While the middle-aged Cuban man steered against the powerful northerly currents, a huge cigar clamped between his teeth, Michael kept a pair of borrowed binoculars trained on the horizon.

Molly clung to a railing as the wind ripped at her clothes and tangled her hair. "Any sign of him?"

"Nothing. Raúl's heading south."

Molly's uneasiness mounted. "South? Toward Cuba?"

Michael nodded.

Suddenly dozens of stories flashed through her mind, stories about ill-fated missions against Castro by exiles fanatical in their patriotism and their determination to reclaim their homeland. "Michael?"

He slowly lowered the binoculars and turned toward her, his expression grim.

"You don't believe he went fishing today, do you?"

"I hope to God I'm wrong, but no."

"But surely he wouldn't . . ."

9

"He would," Michael said tersely. "The god-damned fool would. He's been involved with some underground paramilitary group for years. I looked into them once for Tía Pilar. I decided they were harmless enough, not like Alpha Sixty-six or *Comandos L.*"

Molly recognized the names of two of the most active organizations reputed to carry out terrorist bombings and other clandestine operations against Castro and his supporters. She shuddered to think of the implications had he belonged to one of those. Another group she'd heard of, the one Michael hadn't mentioned, was Brigade 2506, made up of men who had survived the ill-fated Bay of Pigs invasion in 1961. Revered by exiles, the Bay of Pigs veterans claimed to be no longer involved in commando raids, though one of its most prominent members continued to operate a training camp in the county.

"Dammit," Michael swore. "I thought that eventually he would see that there are better ways to end Castro's dictatorship, especially with the fall of communism in the rest of the world."

"But why now, after all this time?" Molly said, unable to imagine the sheer folly of what Michael was suggesting. "You must be wrong. I'm sure he just got caught in a squall or something. He wouldn't try to invade Cuba on his own, for heaven's sakes."

"You don't understand what it's been like

for him. You can't. Not even I fully understand it. Cuba—the Cuba he remembers, anyway—is in his soul. It's as if some vital part of him has been carved away. Whenever new exiles come, he always meets with them, soaking up their news of Cuba like a sponge. For days afterward, his melancholy deepens."

The sadness, Molly thought. That explained the sorrow that perpetually shadowed Tío Miguel's eyes. And Michael was right. His heartache was something she had no way of fully comprehending. She had always lived in her homeland, and even though she no longer lived in Virginia where she'd grown up, she could go back anytime she wished.

"Would he have gone alone, though?" she asked. "Wouldn't there have been others?"

"More than likely, though Raúl says he has heard nothing of such plans. Such men operate in secret, but there is almost always gossip."

As the boat churned through the choppy waters, they emerged beneath bluer skies. The wind settled into little more than a breeze that barely stirred the humid tropical air. But even with the improved weather, the tension didn't lessen as the afternoon wore on.

The one question Molly didn't dare to ask was whether Raúl would risk carrying them all the way into Cuban waters. Nor was she sure she wanted to know whether Michael would allow him to do any less. Fortunately, with nothing but open water in all directions, Molly had no real sense of how close she might be to having both questions answered. Cuba was ninety-six miles from Key West, a hundred and fifty miles from Miami. Unused to nautical speed, she couldn't even be sure how long it would take them to cover that distance.

For all she knew there was little purpose to the zigzagging course they seemed to be on as the summer sun slipped below the horizon in a blaze of orange.

"There!" Michael said eventually, gesturing to Raúl as he kept his binoculars pinned on some tiny speck in the dimming light of a July sunset.

To Molly the boat in the distance was indistinguishable from dozens of others they had seen since leaving the marina. Only as they drew closer did she realize that the boat's engine was still, that its movement was propelled by no more than the drifting currents.

"Tío! Tío Miguel!"

Michael's shouts carried across the water as they pulled alongside the boat. *Niña Pilar* had been painted on the boat's bow in neat, bright-blue letters, a jaunty tribute to a woman Molly couldn't imagine Tío Miguel leaving behind.

"Can you get any closer?" Michael asked Raúl.

"Sí," he said, maneuvering until the boats were touching.

Michael threw a rope across, then looped it through the railing of his uncle's boat until the two were pontooned together. Only then did he leap from Raúl's boat to the deck of his uncle's.

Molly's breath caught in her throat as he made his way carefully from bow to stern. She nearly panicked when he disappeared inside the cabin and failed to return. She had one hand on the railing and was preparing to leap herself, when she heard the boat's engine chug to life, then sputter off again. So, then, Molly thought in dismay, it hadn't been a breakdown. Dear heaven, where was he?

Finally Michael reappeared.

"Michael?" she said softly, her heart hammering as she tried to read the expression on his face.

He swallowed hard before he finally lifted his gaze to meet hers.

"He's gone," he said bleakly. "The inflatable raft is missing, too. I can't tell about life vests, because I'm not certain how many he carried."

"You're sure he's gone back to Cuba, though? Maybe the boat ran out of gas and he took the dinghy to get help," she said, searching desperately for another explanation, even one that flew in the face of the sound she'd just heard of the engine running perfectly smoothly. "Maybe another fisherman picked him up."

"The boat's fine. Besides, he would never

have left it behind," Michael replied with certainty. "We are in Cuban waters, or at least what they view as Cuban waters." He looked to Raúl for confirmation. The fisherman nodded.

"What does that mean?" Molly asked.

"It means the Cuban government extends their territorial rights a couple of miles farther into the waters than international law usually dictates." He sighed with obvious frustration. "Dammit, what has he done? Did he think he could get away with slipping into Cuba? The soldiers will shoot him on sight, either mistaking him for a rafter trying to escape or, if he is armed, seeing him for what he is, an enemy of Castro."

Raúl greeted Michael's announcement with a barrage of Spanish. He hurriedly sketched a cross over his chest, his gaze flashing toward heaven. Though she could understand only about one word in ten, something in the fisherman's voice told Molly he disagreed with Michael's interpretation.

Michael questioned him in impatient, rapid-fire Spanish.

"What?" Molly said. "Michael, what is he saying?"

"Estás loco," Michael said derisively to the other man. *"No es posible."*

"Sí," Raúl said just as adamantly.

"What, dammit?" Molly said, shouting over the pair of them.

14

Michael finally looked at her. "Raúl seems to think it is not possible that my uncle went back to Cuba. He says he would have taken his boat all the way to shore if that had been his intention. He would have tried to land on the beach, not taken a chance crossing the strong currents between here and there in a tiny inflatable raft."

Molly found herself agreeing with Raúl's logic. "Then what does he think happened?"

"He thinks he was murdered," he said in a clipped tone.

"Murdered?" Molly repeated, unable to keep the shock from her voice.

Michael waved a hand dismissively. "You see why I say he is crazy. Who would want to murder an old man who has never done anything to hurt anyone in his life?"

To Molly the passionate disagreements of the exiles had always seemed incomprehensible, but she knew that emotions ran high. Murder was not out of the question, given the right circumstances.

"Can you dismiss what he is saying so easily?" she asked gently, though she didn't want to believe Raúl's theory any more than Michael did. "You're a homicide detective, Michael. You of all people know how important it is to look beyond the obvious. You know that people can be driven to kill for reasons that make no sense to anyone else."

He glared at her. "Maybe just this once I

15

don't want to think like a detective,'' he snapped. ''Maybe just this once I don't want to know anything about someone who might be sick enough to hurt an old man.''

She understood his desperation, felt something akin to it herself, and yet clinging to an illusion wouldn't help them to find answers. ''I know you, Michael. You won't rest until you know the truth. Not about something as important as this.''

A sigh shuddered through him then. He slid his sunglasses back into place, shading his eyes, though it was long past any need for them. Without another word he secured Tío Miguel's boat to be towed back to Miami, then gestured to Raúl.

''Wait,'' Molly said. ''Couldn't we take the boat back?''

He shook his head. ''I don't want to chance destroying any evidence that might be on board.'' He again gestured for Raúl to begin heading home.

The fishing boat turned to the north and began chugging through the swift currents of the Florida straits. Molly could no longer read Michael's expression in the darkness closing in around them, but he stood facing south—toward his homeland. Toward Cuba.

CHAPTER
TWO

Hours later, by the time the silent trio reached the marina again, Metro-Dade evidence technicians were waiting at the dock, summoned by Michael over Raúl's ship-to-shore radio. Once again Michael leapt aboard his uncle's boat, started the engine, and guided it the last hundred yards into its slip. As soon as the fishing boat was secured, the sleepy, out-of-uniform evidence techs—Ken Marshall and Felipe Domínguez—joined Michael on deck. When Molly made a move to join them, Michael waved her back.

"I want them treating this like a crime scene," he said grimly. "There's no point in adding another set of prints or messing up what's already here. If you'll wait at the restaurant, I'll call a cab for you in a minute."

Molly shook her head. "I'm going to make a phone call, but I'm not leaving."

He opened his mouth, clearly intending to argue, then shrugged. "Fine. I'll give you a lift when we're through."

At the pay phone inside the restaurant, she called her ex-husband. He was not going to appreciate the fact that she was calling at what he would consider the middle of the night or that she hadn't called much earlier. She shrugged off his displeasure. Hal never approved of much she did anyway. He could just add this to the list.

"Where the hell are you?" Hal DeWitt demanded. "I thought you were picking Brian up at eight o'clock. It's the goddamned middle of the night."

She almost laughed at the predictable response. Instead, she managed to sound dutifully contrite. "I'm sorry. I couldn't get to a phone before now."

"The woman who keeps a cellular phone attached to her eardrum?" he retorted with derision.

"Hal, is this really necessary?"

"I think it is." When that was met with silence, he added, "Okay, okay. When are you getting here?"

"I'm not. I really need you to keep Brian another day or so."

That was greeted with his most put-upon sigh. "Couldn't you have called earlier? He

18

could have been in bed by now. You haven't gotten yourself mixed up in another goddamn murder, have you?" he inquired sarcastically.

The last three homicide cases in which Molly had inadvertently become entangled had irritated the daylights out of her ex-husband. He'd acted as if she personally had been responsible for the deaths. He also made it seem as if she'd done it only to aggravate him.

"No," she said, refusing to accept the possibility that Tío Miguel might be dead or to be drawn into an argument. "But a friend of mine is in the middle of a family emergency. I'd like to be able to help out. It'll be easier if Brian stays with you."

Since leaving Brian with him more often was exactly what Hal had been pleading with Molly to do, she guessed he wouldn't dare deny the request, though he'd do his best to make her feel guilty in the meantime.

"I suppose it'll be okay," he said grudgingly.

She bit back a sarcastic retort about his enthusiasm. Instead, her tone deliberately mild, she said only, "Thanks. Since he's still up anyway, let me speak with him, please."

To her amazement, Hal didn't argue. Maybe he didn't want to know what friend she was helping. He wasn't fond of her best friend, Liza Hastings, and he was downright hostile about Michael. A few seconds later, Brian was on the line.

"Hey, Mom, what's up?"

19

"I've asked your dad if you can stay with him another night or two. He's agreed."

"How come?"

She didn't want to alarm him about Tío Miguel's disappearance until they knew more. "It's already late and Michael's tied up for a while, so I can't get home. You might as well get a decent night's sleep."

"Oh."

She picked up on his unenthusiastic tone of voice. "You okay with that? Is everything all right at your dad's?"

"I suppose."

It was an amazingly reticent answer for a kid who was never at a loss for words. "Brian? What's going on?"

"He's got this lady here," he finally blurted. "She keeps looking at me like she wishes I'd get lost."

Molly was surprised. Hal had always been careful not to have his dates around when Brian visited, perhaps to give the illusion that he was still pining away for Molly. For a time anyway, he had been, or so he'd claimed. However, they'd resolved all of that months ago. Apparently he'd finally accepted that they had no future and moved on with his life. Brian was normally just fine with that in theory, possibly because he adored Michael and hoped that something would develop between him and Molly. In fact, he'd done everything up to and including personally proposing marriage to Michael on Molly's behalf. Molly had been horrified. Michael had taken it in stride. He'd had a man-to-man talk with Brian, taken his concerns seriously, and promised to keep the suggestion in mind.

Obviously, unlike Michael, this particular woman hadn't done anything to ingratiate herself with Brian. Apparently she didn't understand the value of having a precocious kid in her corner.

"Don't worry about her," Molly advised. "Your dad wants you there, and that's all that matters. I'll talk to you sometime tomorrow."

"What about summer school? I'll probably be really tired anyway, since it's so late. Do I get to stay home?" he inquired hopefully.

"Not a chance. I know you stay awake playing video games until this hour, when you think I'm already asleep. You'll get by."

"But dad's never taken me to school before."

"Your dad knows the way. He'll drop you off."

"But my homework's at home."

Molly had to hold back a chuckle at this one last try. Homework was not something uppermost on Brian's mind most of the time. "Tell your dad to stop off at the condo so you can pick it up," she advised him.

"Okay," he said, accepting defeat gracefully.

"See you, Mom. Tell Michael hi for me. Has he asked you to marry him yet?"

"No, Brian, and he never will if you keep on pestering him about it." She thought about the implications of her response and quickly amended, "Not that I want him to, anyway."

"Yeah, right," Brian teased.

"Bye, kiddo. Behave yourself."

When she'd hung up, Molly walked back to the dock. She leaned against a piling, hoping that just watching the investigation going on on the boat might spark a few theories of her own about what might have happened to Tío Miguel.

As she waited, Raúl once again unloaded the cooler filled with his day's catch. When he caught sight of her, he went back aboard and brought her a rusty lawn chair that had been stored in the cabin, apparently for family outings on the nearby beaches.

"Sit," he instructed her.

Even though the chair had clearly been the victim of too much salt air, it was better than continuing to stand indefinitely. "Thank you."

She studied the middle-aged Cuban, wondering how much English he spoke and understood. He and Michael had spoken only Spanish in her presence. "Raúl, do you speak English?"

"*Sí*, I speak some English," he said haltingly.

"Why do you believe someone harmed Miguel?"

Something that might have been fear darkened his eyes. He shook his head, muttering, "*No comprendo*, señorita."

Molly's knowledge of Spanish was too limited for explaining the complexities of her question. Besides, she had a feeling that Raúl understood her perfectly well. Something about Miguel's disappearance, however, frightened him.

She tried again, hoping to take a more innocuous route to the same information. "Was he alone this morning?"

"*No sé.*"

"You don't know?" she said disbelievingly. "I thought you saw him."

"*Sí.*"

"But you saw no one else?"

He shrugged.

This was getting her nowhere fast. Either he had seen someone and that someone had terrified him into having a convenient memory lapse or he was implying that someone could have been hiding belowdecks on Miguel's boat or on another boat that had followed Miguel to sea or . . . Hell, his vague response could have meant almost anything. Molly sighed.

Raúl regarded her worriedly. "The señorita would like something to drink?" he asked, suddenly finding his English vocabulary.

"No, thank you."

"I have very good rum."

"No."

"Beer?"

Molly regarded him evenly. "Nothing."

He backed away then and picked up his cooler and fishing gear. As he started down the dock, he hesitated. "I am sorry, señorita."

"That's okay, Raúl. You'll call Señor O'Hara if you think of anything, right?"

He bobbed his head. "*Sí, sí*, I will call."

Molly figured Michael shouldn't hold his breath expecting evidence from this particular source, whether he was a friend of Miguel's or not.

She glanced back at the *Niña Pilar* and wondered what was going on belowdecks. What could they find? Fingerprints? On a charter fishing boat wouldn't that be like hoping to use prints to ID a killer in the crowd at Joe Robbie Stadium? Even though Tío Miguel was a fanatic about cleaning up his boat, who knew how many sets of prints could have been scattered around the cabin and on deck since the last time he'd polished everything. Maybe Michael was hoping to find some suspicious piece of evidence, a piece of cloth snagged from someone's shirt, a button, traces of blood indicating a struggle.

The thought of the latter sent a shiver down Molly's spine. Just as she'd anticipated, Michael wasn't likely to ignore any possibility, no matter how absurd or terrifying he personally thought it to be. His success as a homicide detective was based on his gut instincts and his cool, meticulous attention to detail. He would bring that same skill to bear on an investigation of his uncle's mysterious disappearance, no matter how difficult it might be for him to remain objective. If anything, he would be more relentless and thorough than usual.

He was still grim faced when he finally emerged nearly an hour later. He looked dismayed when he saw her, as if he'd completely forgotten her existence. It was an understandable reaction, but hardly flattering.

"Sorry," he said. "We'll be able to leave soon."

"Don't apologize. Have you found anything?"

He shook his head. "Not a damn thing. Oh, there are plenty of prints, but who knows how long they've been around."

"Any signs that he might have struggled with someone?"

"Nothing."

Molly had a sudden thought. "What about a gun?"

"If he owns one, he took it with him."

"A map of Cuba?"

"He knows those waters and that shoreline like the back of his hand. He wouldn't have needed one." He muttered a curse in Spanish. "We couldn't find one damned thing to indicate what he might have been up to out there besides fishing."

"His gear was still aboard, then?"

"All of it, as far as I could tell."

"Had he caught anything today?"

"What the hell difference . . ." Michael began, then grinned. He leaned down and planted a kiss on her forehead. "Molly, you're a genius. If he caught anything, then this was just another fishing trip. I'll be back in a minute."

He jumped aboard the *Niña Pilar* and headed for the stern of the boat, which was apparently where Miguel kept ice-filled coolers for the day's catch. When he came back, his expression was even more somber than before.

"Any fish?"

He shook his head. "But there is melting ice in one cooler as if he'd expected to fill it with fish. Another has ice and beer and a couple of sandwiches. I didn't see any empty bottles. Whatever happened must have happened right after he got out there."

"What do you think that means?"

"I think it means that Raúl could have been right," he admitted with obvious reluctance. "Someone could have forced him off that boat. He wouldn't have headed for Cuba in an inflatable raft without any provisions. Even from where we found his boat, he was hours from shore depending on the currents. Hell, from what I know about the water in the straits, he would have been a goddamned fool to abandon his boat there and head for Cuba on a raft. He'd have been fighting the currents all the way. The rafters leaving Cuba count on those currents to take them north to America, not south."

"Will you tell your aunt that?"

For the first time in all the months she had known the extraordinarily confident detective, Molly saw genuine uncertainty in Michael's eyes.

"I don't know," he said quietly. "I don't know what the hell to say to her. I don't want to alarm her, but . . ."

"Michael, she's already alarmed, I'm sure. She'd have to be. I think you have to concentrate on what's being done to find him, rather than on all the things you don't know."

"Like what? I don't even know where to start," he said angrily. "I'm a cop and I don't have the vaguest idea where to begin."

Molly refused to believe that. "Nonsense. At the moment, you're thinking like a grief-stricken nephew. As soon as you begin thinking like a policeman, you'll know exactly what to do next, what you'd do if this were any other suspicious disappearance."

He shot her a wry look. "I gather from that that you have an idea yourself that you're assuming will come to me once I begin to think clearly. Feel free to share it. I'm coming up blank, and right this minute I will do almost anything, no matter how farfetched, to postpone going to my aunt's house without answers."

"Call *Hermanos al Rescate*," she suggested, referring to a group of pilots whose name in English meant Brothers to the Rescue. The organization had been formed to try to save at least some of the desperate people who tried to flee Cuba on makeshift rafts. In one recent year over 2,500 people had made the attempt in everything from inner tubes to glued-together Styrofoam. *Hermanos al Rescate* found 103 of these foolhardy, courageous people in its first two years. Molly recalled that they had also found 44 empty rafts between the beaches of Varadero and Mariel and the Florida Keys. It was not an especially cheering statistic. She concentrated on emphasizing the positive.

"I know they usually conduct their searches looking for rafters heading from Cuba to Miami," Molly added, "but I'm sure they'd help look for your uncle, and they're used to flying over those waters looking for tiny specks on the sea. Combined with a Coast Guard search, wouldn't that help to reassure your aunt, at least for now, that everything possible is being done to find Miguel?"

Michael sighed heavily, obviously every bit as aware of the statistics as she was. "At least I'll be able to tell her that people will be looking for Tío Miguel in the morning," he agreed finally. "I know one of the pilots. I'll call him."

Molly was determined to keep prodding him with ideas until his own instincts kicked in. "Shouldn't you call the State Department and see if there have been any incidents along the Cuban beaches?"

He shook his head. "We'll know soon enough if there have been. Castro just loves to carry on about these imperialist attacks on his sovereign shores. In the meantime, I don't want to stir things up in Washington and have them breathing down my aunt's neck for information about his illegal plotting to invade Cuba. It's a violation of the Neutrality Act. Washington issues warnings periodically just to prevent the exile groups from acting on their wild ideas."

"And when the commandos do it anyway, half the time Washington winks and looks the other way," Molly pointed out.

"Only if no one raises a fuss about it. No, I'll handle this myself."

"What about work?"

"I'll take leave time. God knows, I have plenty of it built up. I haven't taken a vacation day off in years."

"Have you officially reported your uncle as missing?"

Michael shook his head.

"How'd you get the evidence techs here, then?"

"Called in a favor," he admitted. "Look, I'm going to make that call to try to get those rescue flights in the air in the morning. At least I can pinpoint where we picked up the boat. It'll give them a starting point for the search. If Ken and

Felipe get finished inside, ask them to wait for me.''

Molly nodded. She wanted to shadow him, but knew he would be infuriated by the overly protective gesture. She was surprised he'd tolerated her staying around as long as he had. Any second now she expected him to insist on her returning home. To which she intended to reply that he'd have to haul her out of his wagon kicking and screaming. It wouldn't do a lot for his image as a cool, unemotional cop. She figured he'd grasp the improbability of shaking her loose fairly readily, once she'd explained her intentions to him.

In the meantime, since the search of the boat was pretty much complete, maybe she could sneak in a quick peek before Michael returned to forbid it. She actually made it as far as the aft deck before she heard footsteps behind her.

''Going someplace?'' Michael inquired.

''Just taking a look around,'' she admitted. ''Your guys are almost through so I won't be disturbing any evidence now, right?''

''And you honestly think you might spot something that two well-trained evidence technicians missed?''

''You never know.''

He gazed toward heaven with a familiar pleading expression, then sighed. ''Fine. Look to your heart's content. I'll check with the guys, and then we're out of here.''

Unfortunately, Michael's smug attitude appeared to be justified. Molly couldn't discover one single clue to explain Miguel's disappearance. She did, however, hear an odd noise coming from beneath the stacks of life preservers in a built-in wooden storage bin. The faint but unmistakable ticking gave her goose bumps.

It was an unusual place to hide a clock, unless said clock was attached to a timing device. She'd seen enough movies to suspect that a crude bomb could be every bit as effective as one made by professional terrorists.

"Michael!" Molly shouted at the top of her lungs, all the while inching away from the sound.

Three policeman responded to the panic in her voice. She pointed toward the sound. "In there. A bomb, I think."

"Don't be ridiculous," Michael said, just as Ken Marshall gently lifted out first one orange life vest, then another.

"Holy shit!" he murmured, his freckled complexion turning even more pale. "Let's get the hell off this tub and get the bomb squad down here."

The four of them clambered onto the dock. While the crisply efficient Marshall called for backup, Michael and Domínguez went up and down the slips to make sure there was no one in the nearby boats.

"I'm taking the boat out," Michael announced.

31

"No way, man," Domínguez countered, blocking his way. Shorter than Michael and built more squarely, he looked like a bulldog confronting a sleek, angry Doberman. "You'd have to be *loco* to get anywhere near that bomb."

"I'm not endangering other people," Michael insisted stubbornly. "Who knows how powerful the damn thing is or when it's set to go off."

"Exactly my point," the evidence tech said, trying to hold Michael back. "Let those crazies who like to live on the edge deal with this. That's what the county pays them for."

"It's my responsibility," Michael insisted, breaking free of the other policeman's grasp.

When Molly started to follow him, Felipe Domínguez held her back, his determined grip on her arm almost painful. "You won't stop him, and he sure as hell won't want you with him."

She knew it was useless to fight him, knew that he was right. Biting back a sob, she whispered, "But what if . . ."

The policeman cursed at the sound of the engine coming to life. "Jesus, O'Hara," he muttered as the boat began to move.

"Michael!" Molly shouted over the steady throbbing of the engine. Bile rose in her throat and tears stung her eyes as the boat inched away from the dock.

Just then Ken Marshall returned, saw the moving boat and stared after it, openmouthed with shock. "Mother of God, Felipe, why didn't you stop him?"

Felipe turned his anguished dark-eyed gaze on his colleague. "How? You know what O'Hara's like when he gets something into his head. Did you want me to handcuff him?"

"If that's what it took," Ken snapped in exasperation.

"What time is it?" Molly asked with a dawning sense of horror and a sudden understanding of what the whole day's events could have been about. Her hands were shaking so badly she couldn't see the face of her watch.

"Just before midnight."

"Exactly, dammit!"

"Eleven fifty-eight. Why?"

She lifted her hands helplessly. "I don't know. Just a feeling I have."

"That the bomb would be set for midnight," Ken guessed.

She shook her head. "One minute after."

Both men regarded her with puzzlement. "Why?"

"The date," she said with certainty, her voice choked. "It'll be the anniversary of the goddamned Cuban revolution."

They could already hear sirens in the background as Ken kept his gaze riveted on the second hand of his watch. "Eleven fifty-nine," he breathed. Then, "Midnight."

The next sixty seconds were the longest of

33

Molly's life. Her heart was in her throat. The boat was a couple of hundred yards into the bay and still chugging toward open water.

"Twelve-oh-one," Ken said.

Molly's eyes burned from tears and from straining to see through the darkness. There was no mistaking the sudden spark of fire at the back of the boat, the puff of smoke.

"Oh, God," she murmured, wanting to turn away, but unable to. Her gaze was fixed on the *Niña Pilar* with a sort of horrified fascination. Waiting. Waiting.

Just when she thought she could bear the terrible suspense not one second longer, flames shot into the air with an explosion of sound that slammed through the stillness and echoed in her head. One of the policemen, she had no idea which one, gathered her close, rocking her back and forth, even as a steady stream of curses spewed from his mouth.

"Michael?" she whispered, weeping. She looked up into Ken Marshall's stricken face. "Where is he? Did he get off?"

"Even if he did . . ." Felipe began, before Ken shushed him.

Molly didn't need to hear the rest of the words. Even if Michael had gotten off the boat, what were the odds that he was far enough away when the billowing flames danced across the water?

CHAPTER
THREE

The music at Sundays by the Bay trailed off, replaced by screams and the pounding of footsteps as people raced from the restaurant toward the dock, awed by the fireball spreading across the water. Molly clung to Ken Marshall, her gaze riveted on the water, haphazard bits of old, familiar prayers whirling through her head.

"The Lord is my Shepherd . . ."

"Our Father who art in heaven . . ."

"Now I lay me down to sleep . . ."

No one prayer was ever finished before the next took its place, as if her brain was trying to find the one prayer that could magically make this come out right.

When she could finally tear her gaze away, she looked up into Ken Marshall's brimming eyes, eyes that had no doubt seen their share of terrible scenes but nothing so horrifying as this. Domínguez was standing beside them, stone faced. Only his black-as-onyx eyes reflected the same kind of agony that churned inside Molly. She realized that in calling these two particular policemen earlier, Michael had not just called in favors, he had recruited friends. And these friends were every bit as shaken as she was.

"You have to send somebody after him," she pleaded. "He could be out there, hurt."

"It's not safe, not yet," Ken Marshall responded bluntly. "But we'll find him, I promise you that. We've got paramedics and Coast Guard rescuers pouring in here." His expression softened and his voice turned gentle and cajoling, the kind of voice people used on someone whose state of mind was rightly considered as fragile as spun glass. "Why don't we go up to the restaurant and get you something to drink?"

Molly shook her head. "I'm not leaving here, not until Michael is back."

She heard someone in the crowd offer to bring her coffee, and a moment later a warm cup was placed in her trembling hands. She automatically lifted it to her lips and took a sip of the strong black brew, though her eyes never left the water. Several people who'd apparently been drinking in the bar or having a late meal before going home climbed aboard their boats and turned high-beam searchlights onto the water to aid the rescuers.

Molly had understood Ken Marshall's blunt words. She knew it wouldn't be safe until the last of the flames had burned themselves out, but with every second that passed, her terror mounted. Images passed through her mind, each one more horrifying than the one before. Michael could have been killed outright in the explosion. Or thrown clear of the boat, unconscious, only to drown. Or while plunging into the sea, he could have been coated with the boat's fuel, then turned into a human torch.

She moaned softly, tears coursing down her cheeks. There were so many things she'd never told Michael. She'd never admitted how much stronger she was, thanks to him. Nor how much he meant to her. Was it too late? In that one blinding instant had they been robbed of a future that had promised to be something incredibly special?

"Will you be okay?" Marshall asked, hunkering down beside her as she huddled in the chair Raúl had left for her. "I want to join the search."

She glanced around. Domínguez had already gone, easing away without Molly's even noticing. "Please, go," she said. "Find him."

As she waited for some word, Molly was distantly aware of the arrival of sleepy overnight crews from some of the local television stations. Thankfully none of the reporters seemed to be aware of her or her connection to the bombing story. She couldn't have formed a coherent thought for them right now.

"Molly?"

She glanced up into the worried face of Ted Ryan, a reporter from the morning paper. He'd been assigned to cover some of the same homicide cases that Molly had unofficially investigated. She'd been trying to save her own neck or that of a friend. Ted had provided a more objective eye. He was bright and ambitious, which meant he'd be dogging her with questions regardless of her fragile emotional state.

"Not now," she said in the slim hope it would send him on to more forthcoming sources.

He slid his notebook and pen into the back pocket of his rumpled khaki pants, possibly to indicate that his questions were personal, rather than professional. Molly knew better than to trust him or any journalist on the trail of inside information.

"Was this some sort of film stunt?" he asked.

Though it was a natural enough question given her profession as an assistant in the Metro-Dade film office, Molly felt like laughing hysterically. If only that was all it had been, a crazy, dangerous movie stunt in which everyone lived except the fictional bad guy.

"No," she said finally, shivering at the memory of Tío Miguel's boat splintering into a million burning pieces with Michael most likely still aboard. "This was the real thing."

Ted nodded as if he'd already guessed as much. "I heard a cop was on that boat right before it blew. Since you're here and it wasn't a movie stunt, I'm guessing the cop was O'Hara," he said, his voice surprisingly subdued. His gaze strayed to the water as if he couldn't quite bear to meet her eyes.

Molly saw no point in denying it. "Yes," she whispered.

To her surprise, Ted's expression registered genuine dismay. He squeezed her hand sympathetically. "I'm sorry. I know he and I are usually at odds, but I liked him. He was a great cop."

The past tense infuriated her. "*Is* a great cop, dammit! He is not dead."

Ted looked miserable. "God, I'm sorry. I didn't mean to make it worse. Look, is there anything I can do for you?"

"Not unless you can get out there and find him for me."

"I'll go see if there's any word yet," he said, then scurried off as if he couldn't wait to get away from her and the deeply personal pain she didn't even try to hide. At least he hadn't plagued her with questions about the explosion or what had led up to it. She supposed she should be grateful for that much consideration. And she knew that Ted would do nothing to betray her role in this story to his rivals. He was too much of a fierce competitor for that. So for the moment she could sit where she was, alone and anonymous, waiting for word.

It seemed like hours, though it was probably no more than a half hour or sixty minutes, before she finally heard a triumphant shout echo across the water. She stood on unsteady legs and made her way down the dock. Pushing her way through the crowd, she finally spotted a Coast Guard boat speeding toward shore. Paramedics, hauling a stretcher and carrying other critical equipment, rushed through the crowd. When they tried to get Molly to move aside, she stubbornly refused.

"It's okay," Felipe Domínguez told the paramedics, edging in beside her. He put a bracing arm around her waist and pulled her forward. "She was here with O'Hara."

She looked into his troubled eyes. "They've found him, haven't they?"

"*Sí,*" he said quietly. He moved his hand to her shoulder and gave her a reassuring squeeze. "They say he's alive, but they have said no more than that, not to me, anyway."

She glanced at the paramedics. "Did they radio in anything about his condition?"

At a nod from Felipe, the dark-haired, tanned paramedic who seemed to be in charge told her, "He's got a nasty bump on the side of his head. He was unconscious when they found him, bobbing along in his life vest."

With Felipe's hand continuing to rest gently on her shoulder, Molly finally faced the most agonizing question of all. Trying to contain a shudder, she asked, "Was he burned?"

"No, ma'am. The explosion threw him in the opposite direction from the worst of the fire. Sounds to me like he might have been about to dive off the bow, when that sucker blew. He's one lucky son of a bitch." At a scowl from his partner, he winced. "Sorry, ma'am."

Molly was too intent on the activity at the end of the pier to worry about the paramedic's language. As the Coast Guard cutter docked, she choked back the sobs that threatened. Holding her breath, she watched as they carried Michael off the boat and lowered him onto the stretcher. His clothes were ripped and singed. They had stripped away his life vest and shirt on the Coast Guard boat and already an IV line was in place. There were gashes on his forehead and arms and his complexion was far too pale, but she could detect the steady rise and fall of his chest. The paramedics didn't fight her as she knelt beside him and clung to his icy, lifeless hand.

"Damn you, Michael O'Hara, you'd better not die on me," she whispered furiously.

Either her words or the tears that spilled onto his bare chest apparently got through to him. His eyelids flickered and his lips tried to curve into a smile. "I'm not going to die, *que-*

rida," he murmured. "Too much unfinished business."

"The explosion," she said with an air of resignation. "And Tío Miguel."

He gave an almost imperceptible shake of his head. "You and me."

● ● ●

They tried to admit Michael at county-run Jackson Memorial Hospital so they could watch him overnight and through the following day. Unfortunately, there weren't enough doctors and nurses in the entire University of Miami-affiliated trauma center to hold him down once he'd made up his mind to go.

"Michael, I will go to see your family," Molly promised in what she guessed was probably a vain attempt to get him to listen to reason. "I will tell them everything that's happened. I've already told them most of it on the phone and convinced them they don't need to rush over here in the middle of the night."

She didn't mention that it had taken all of her persuasive skills to accomplish that. Tío Pedro had been ready to pack the entire family into the car, along with a priest, when she finally got through to him that Michael would more than likely be released first thing in the morning anyway. That might be only a couple of hours away, but she figured those hours were best spent in a hospital bed, not chasing down clues in his uncle's disappearance and the bombing of the fishing boat. She tried one more time to make him see reason.

"You'll think much more clearly after a couple of hours of rest. You won't get that at home with everyone hovering over you. Besides, you have no business leaving the hospital. You've just been through a major trauma."

"A couple of scratches," he argued.

"And a knock on the head that's obviously addled your brain," she countered.

He sat up, wincing with the effort. "This is something I have to do, *amiga*. Will you help me or not?"

Molly glanced at the harried resident trauma surgeon, who shrugged. "If he goes, it's against medical advice, but I can't stop him. If he's not staying, I've got two gunshot wounds out there who are in far greater need of my help."

"By all means, treat your other patients," Michael said with a dismissive wave of his hand. He winced in pain, but remained stubbornly determined. "Molly, find my clothes."

"Your clothes are a little the worse for wear," she reminded him. "They're ripped and soaking wet. I could bring clothes from home in the morning."

"I'll walk out of here stark naked if I have to," he warned.

So much for that. "An interesting possibility," she commented. "That ought to guarantee catching the attention of the nurses. Maybe one of them will convince you to stay.''

He scowled at her.

"Okay. Okay," Molly muttered, giving up. "I think I saw some jeans and a T-shirt wadded up in the back of your wagon, along with all the soccer gear. I'll go get 'em. Meantime, sit still, please. This could be the last rest you get for a while, if you can call it that."

"Are Felipe and Ken out there?"

"Half the Metro-Dade police force is out there. The rest of them are on the Bay picking up debris, hoping to piece together some decent evidence. You created quite a commotion, Detective."

"Tell Felipe and Ken I need to talk to them."

"Your boss will be disappointed if he's not in on your powwow."

"Okay, fine. Send him in, too."

"Maybe you should just go into the lobby and hold a damned press conference," she said irritably, as the tight band of tension around her head finally snapped. She started to the door of the treatment room.

"Molly?"

She turned.

"You okay?"

"Sure. I'm just dandy," she retorted. "You get yourself practically blown to smithereens and now it's back to business as usual. You'll have to pardon me if I can't switch emotional gears as quickly as you do."

He eased gingerly off the examining table. "Come here."

"What for?"

"Come on, *amiga,* humor me."

She walked slowly over to him. Her insides were still turning somersaults. He cupped her face in both hands and tilted her head until she was forced to meet his gaze.

"It's over now and I'm okay," he said quietly.

A sigh eased through her, but relief was tantalizingly elusive. Molly slid her arms around Michael's waist and rested her head against his chest. He felt warm and solid and very much alive. If she could have held on like this forever, it might have reassured her. Instead, she knew deep down that this respite would be short-lived. If anything, the real danger was just beginning.

CHAPTER
FOUR

Outside the doors of the relatively new trauma center entrance, the media hounds were gathered like a pack of irritable wolves. Before Molly went through those doors, she found a police spokesman. He was clearly a rookie, judging by his age and the fact that he was hiding inside, rather than outside where he could hobnob with the reporters. She pulled him aside and suggested that this might be the perfect time for some sort of statement.

"Who are you?" he asked suspiciously. "Do you work for the hospital?"

"No, but I have to get something from O'Hara's car for him and I really don't want to be the one they start questioning out there. It'd be a lot better if you gave them an update, something official."

"But nobody's issued anything formal yet," the officer argued.

This was definitely not a man inclined to climb out on a limb. "I can solve that problem. Tell them the doctors are impressed with Detective O'Hara's hard head," she suggested.

"Huh?"

The challenge of getting through to him lost its appeal. "Never mind. I'm sure you'll be able to think of something innocuous. That's what people in your line of work are best at."

The officer regarded her uncertainly, clearly not sure whether to take offense at her sarcasm. Since she really wanted him to distract the media —and since she frequently had to do the same kind of public relations tap dance—she apologized.

"Sorry. Just pacify them, okay?"

"I'll get the director."

Obviously this was not a man who craved the limelight. She predicted a very short career in the public information office. "You can forget the director. He's in with O'Hara. You're on your own, Officer."

Just to make sure he didn't turn tail and run, she nudged him out the door ahead of her. As she'd expected, the reporters turned into a frenzied pack, lobbing questions faster than tennis balls flew at the annual Lipton International Tournament over on Key Biscayne.

Since she didn't trust the reticent young

man's ability to satisfy their hunger for information for long, as soon as all attention was focused on him, Molly slipped past the crowd. When she reached Michael's big wagoneer, which she'd left illegally parked and protectively watched over by a willing hospital security guard, she opened the tailgate and collapsed for a moment on the cool metal. All of the tension of the past few hours caught up with her at once.

"Are you okay, ma'am?" the petite female security guard in her snug navy-blue uniform asked.

"Just a delayed reaction."

"How's O'Hara?"

"You know him?" she said, regarding the young African-American woman with surprise. In a hospital complex the size of JMH with its eight thousand or so employees and physicians and its huge daily volume of traffic, she was astonished anyone even remembered the names of their co-workers.

"Sure. He turns up here all the time when probable homicides roll in. That's how I knew it was him. I recognized his car and tag number. The man refuses to park where he's supposed to. You must have got that from him."

"Bad habits do tend to get around."

"So, is he okay? Nobody's come out I could ask. We've got a full moon. The whole damn place is filled up with crazies. Nobody takes a break on a night like this."

"Michael's okay. At any rate, he insists on leaving. I'm supposed to be out here scrounging for clothes for him to wear."

"You sit right where you are. I'll get 'em for you." She scrambled into the back of the wagon, sorted through the clutter of soccer balls and knee pads, and emerged triumphantly clutching a pair of grass-stained jeans and an embarrassingly wrinkled T-shirt. "They're not pretty, but they'll do, right?"

Molly laughed for the first time in hours. "They won't exactly enhance his image as the best-dressed cop on the force."

"He is one slick dude, isn't he?" the guard said, grinning at the comedown from Michael's usual spiffy designer suits. "Serves him right for leaving against advice. That is what he's up to, isn't it?"

"You've got it." Molly took the clothes. "Thanks. We'll no doubt see you shortly."

"Tell him I want this car out of here before shift change or the boss will bust my butt."

"I'll tell him," Molly said. "But I don't think he intends to waste a second more than necessary as a guest of the hospital."

Back inside the treatment room, Molly found Michael trying to persuade Metro-Dade Safety Director Lucas Petty to assign him full-time to investigate the bombing and his uncle's disappearance. The burly black man with his tough, by-the-book philosophy of operating the department wasn't buying Michael's reasoning for an instant.

"Last I checked you were a homicide detective, O'Hara. We've got no body."

"Dammit, my uncle left on that boat. Now he's missing and the boat's been bombed. In my book that adds up to reasonable cause to suspect foul play."

"It surely does," Petty said with a genial nod of agreement. "And I will even go along with the idea that your uncle was taken against his will. You, however, will not be conducting whatever investigation this department decides to launch. You'll be home with your sorry butt resting in bed, like the doctor ordered."

Marshall and Domínguez turned away to keep the public safety director from spotting their commiserating grins. Obviously they knew, as did Molly, that Lucas Petty didn't have a prayer of keeping Michael out of this particular investigation. They all waited for his anticipated declaration of intent.

Sure enough, his jaw set stubbornly, he fumbled in the pocket of his ruined pants, came out with his wallet, and removed his badge. "As of now, I'm on leave."

Petty looked as if he wanted to strangle him. He rocked back on his heels and glared. "You take sick leave, then you'd damned sight better stay home and act sick."

"I'm taking vacation leave."

"Not without prior authorization."

"Don't push me, Lucas," Michael said quietly, his expression lethal.

Unfortunately, Lucas Petty didn't appear to be in any mood to have his buttons pushed either. He took two steps forward until he was in Michael's face. "O'Hara, you are treading on very thin ice here."

Michael never even flinched. "Is my leave granted or not?"

"If it's not?"

"Then I'll quit, dammit. Right here and right now. You'll have a hell of a time explaining to the press why one of your best homicide detectives was forced into early retirement. And forget about any hogwash about a medical disability stemming from this damned explosion. When I'm finished with this investigation, I will transfer into the Miami PD, which has been begging me to do just that for the past ten years, and I will look for every opportunity to make you regret this whole lousy episode."

Petty backed up and threw his hands in the air. "Jesus, O'Hara, you know it's bad news taking on an investigation in which you're emotionally involved."

"You don't have the time or the manpower to give this case the attention it deserves," Michael countered. "Nobody will care more than I do about seeing that it's solved."

Lucas Petty cast his gaze heavenward. Judging from his sour expression when he finally looked back at Michael, he hadn't received any divine inspiration. "Okay, okay, you win. Take your leave. How much time do you want?"

"As long as it takes."

"Terrific. Your fellow officers in homicide will be pleased to take over your work load, I'm sure."

Michael glared at him. "Don't you try to lay a guilt trip on me. I've carried more than my share of work for my entire fifteen years in the department."

Lucas Petty heaved a sigh of resignation. "Yeah, you have. Okay, O'Hara, do what you have to do. Be careful, though. This bombing thing tonight wasn't some amateur prank." He held out his hand and shook Michael's. His expression softened. "I'm glad you're okay, son." He looked at Marshall and Domínguez. "You guys coming?"

They glanced at Michael, who shook his head.

"Not just yet, boss," Marshall replied.

The public safety director's eyes narrowed. "You two aren't on leave. Remember that."

"Yes, sir," Marshall replied, his cheeks flushing with a patch of guilty color.

Domínguez just avoided his gaze.

Petty looked as if he wanted to launch into another lecture, but eventually he just shook his head, muttered something under his breath about maverick cops, and left them alone.

"What do you want us to do?" Felipe Domínguez asked as soon as their boss was gone.

"Ask around on the street, Felipe. I know you have contacts. See what's going on with some of these anti-Castro paramilitary groups. Kenny, when they bring in the remains of the boat, I want you to go over every piece of evidence and tell me exactly what you find. I need to know where to start looking for the people who made that bomb."

Ken Marshall shook his head in disgust. "Exactly how many parts of that bomb do you expect to be recovered from the goddamn bay?"

"One would be enough, if it's the right one, one we can trace."

Domínguez shot him a grin. "Man, you watch too many cop shows on TV. Either that or you've got the soul of some romantic Cuban poet living in a dream world."

Michael grinned back. "I just know what fine, dedicated police officers can come up with when they put their minds to it."

"Oh, man, the pressure," Marshall groaned, but he, too, was grinning now, clearly relieved that Michael was back to his usual bossy behavior, acting as if that explosion had never happened. "You know, O'Hara, one of these days you're going to run the whole damned department. You know exactly how to motivate people."

"Right, pizza and beer at my place at the end of your long, productive days. See you tonight about seven thirty?"

"Tonight?" Domínguez said. "You expect answers tonight?"

"Let's face it, some group out there is going to be very proud of what it did. Most likely they won't be quiet about their accomplishment. My guess is there will be some trumped-up story about Miguel's loyalty to the cause. As for the evidence, if it isn't in the lab today, chances are Kenny's right and it's buried in the muck at the bottom of Biscayne Bay."

● ● ●

To Molly's astonishment, Michael didn't wage a struggle for the keys to his car. After being eased protectively through the crowd of reporters by Marshall and Domínguez, he kidded with the security guard for a moment, then hauled himself into the passenger seat, leaned back, and closed his eyes.

Worried by his ashen complexion, Molly hesitated before turning on the ignition. "You all right?"

"Let's just say I'm glad the kids don't have soccer practice today," he said, referring to the team he coached and on which Molly's son played. "I'm not exactly up to running wind sprints."

"It's not too late to check you in here," she said.

"Not a chance. Most of the people I know who check into this place wind up dead."

"You're a homicide detective," she reminded him as she reluctantly turned on the engine. "You don't come here with folks who are hale and hearty."

"Just drive. I'll be fine." As he said it, he flipped on Spanish-language radio, known for the feverish, generally one-sided, anti-Fidel pitch of its political commentary. It was the first place a terrorist might turn to claim credit for a politically motivated bombing. Molly tried valiantly to pick out distinguishable words from the rapid-fire clip of the newscast. Unfortunately she was lost, even though Spanish classes had left her with at least a serviceable vocabulary.

"Anything?" she asked finally in frustration.

Michael shook his head. "There's mention of the boat blowing up, but no more than that. Perhaps I should go to see Luis myself."

The Luis in question was undoubtedly the controversial news director, Luis Díaz-Nuñez. If Michael was thinking of dropping by the studio, it could only mean he intended to go on the air to stir things up a bit. She could just envision the ensuing on-air shouting match.

"Now?" she asked incredulously. "It is five thirty in the morning. You've just left a hospital . . . you will note that I did not mention that you were not even officially released from said hospital . . . and you're wearing clothes that should have hit the laundry at least a month ago."

"It's radio, *amiga*, not TV."

Molly prayed for patience. "Michael, has it occurred to you that perhaps after the disappearance of your uncle, the bombing of his boat, and a concussion, you might not be thinking too clearly?"

"No," he replied matter-of-factly. He looked at her and grinned. "Okay, I will not go to the radio station now." He glanced out the window for the first time as she turned from Twelfth Avenue onto Seventh Street and headed west into the heart of Little Havana. "Where are you taking me?"

"Where do you think?" she said dryly. "To Tío Miguel's, where everyone has gathered for an all-night vigil. If I don't put you on view in front of the family immediately, they'll just come chasing down to Kendall after you the minute they discover that you're out of the hospital."

She regarded him hopefully. "Maybe we can just do a drive-by-and-wave sort of thing."

He laughed at that. "And Felipe accused me of being a dreamer. You don't think I have the energy to do a radio broadcast, but you figure I can undergo an inspection by my relatives? Wait and see, *amiga*. An hour with Luis would have been child's play by comparison.''

CHAPTER

FIVE

"Castro! I live for the day when I can spit on his grave," Tío Pedro said angrily over the weeping of the three Huerta sisters in Tío Miguel's living room several hours later. It was midmorning and the entire family had been gathered there all through the endless night of waiting.

When Michael and Molly had arrived at dawn, his mother had rushed from the house in her too-large, flowered housedress and matching hot-pink flats. Standing on tiptoe, she had kissed him soundly on both cheeks, then held him at arm's length while she examined him visually from head to toe, clucking at every scratch. There were plenty to cluck over.

Rosa Conchita Huerta was a lovely, petite woman with curling black hair, whose lined face still showed the strain of the years she had stayed behind in Cuba after sending her son to be reared by her sisters in Miami. Her nut-brown eyes followed Michael avidly whenever he was in a room, as if even after all this time, she couldn't make up for the years when he had been out of sight.

Rosa at fifty-five was the youngest of the sisters. Elena, Tío Pedro's wife, was the middle sister. Her round, cheerful face bore none of the lines that kept her younger sister from being truly beautiful. She, too, dressed in bright, flattering colors, even though her figure was no longer girlish. She made no excuses for the fact that she dressed to please her adoring husband and that her abundant figure was the result of sampling too many of the excellent dishes they served in their *Calle Ocho* restaurant.

As for Pilar, the oldest of the Huerta sisters, even on happier occasions she tended to be dressed in somber fabrics and wore her luxuriant black hair pulled back into a well-tamed bun. Her thin, aristocratic face, usually so lovely in repose, had a pinched, haunted look this morning that made her look every one of her sixty-two years. She had managed a watery smile at the sight of Michael, but it was clear she was overcome with grief and worry. Her gaze was fixed on the door and each time it opened, a heartbreaking instant of hope flickered in her eyes, then died at the appearance of each new arrival who was not Miguel.

A half dozen or more of Michael's cousins and as many neighbors were crowded into the minuscule living room. After so many hours on a muggy summer night, the air was stale. Even the chugging air conditioner in the window couldn't seem to cool the room.

Worse from Molly's perspective, the cramped space was filled with so many religious paintings and statues she felt as if she'd wandered into a church rectory. A half-dozen candles were lit in front of a cheap plaster statue of the *La Caridad del Cobre,* the patron saint of Cuba. The candles, each emitting a different perfumed scent, added to the oppressive atmosphere.

Even after Michael had spoken quietly with his aunt for some time, Tía Pilar remained inconsolable, though Molly knew that Michael had kept the two worst-case scenarios to himself. He had told his aunt only that they had found the fishing boat and that his uncle had not been aboard. Molly, too, had tried to reassure the woman that Tío Miguel had no doubt joined another fishing party after his own boat broke down. Tía Pilar had accepted her consoling words with murmured gratitude, but the desolate expression in her eyes never wavered. With the arrival of each neighbor, whether from this Little Havana neighborhood just south of *Calle Ocho* or from her native Cuba, her grief erupted into heartrending sobs.

After a while, feeling like an intruder in the

midst of such openly displayed anguish, Molly had asked to use the phone and gratefully left the cluster of women. In her own family, everyone had been taught to suffer in silence. There would have been no outpouring of grief and, as a result, little comfort offered, since no one ever knew how deeply anyone was affected by loss or illness. As uncomfortable as it made her, she envied Michael's family the ability to let their emotions show. Still, she was glad to have a moment to herself.

The old-fashioned black phone sat on a wobbly table in the hallway, affording Molly little privacy. The sobbing of the women and the passionate arguing of the men provided convenient sound effects for her conversation with her boss. Vince Gates was not going to be overjoyed to be hearing from her two hours after she had been due to arrive at the office. Maybe the background hysteria would convince him that the emergency was real.

"Molly?" he said with an exaggerated air of amazement. "Molly DeWitt? Didn't you used to work here?"

"I thought I still did."

"Then why the hell aren't you here?" he demanded irritably.

"Do you want the short version or the two-hour action-adventure version?"

"I'll take the one that includes your estimated arrival time. I've got Jeannette meeting with a producer who showed up thinking he had an appointment with you.''

Molly swallowed hard. "Sorry. Jeannette will do just fine,'' she reassured him, probably in vain. Vince refused to acknowledge that the Haitian-born clerk was thoroughly overqualified for her entry-level job. He was too worried that she was going to cast some voodoo spell over him, a concern that Jeannette herself did nothing to dispel. In fact, she thoroughly enjoyed taunting him in Creole, managing to inject an ominous note into the most innocuous of words.

"Vince, you know perfectly well Jeannette has worked with me on the last half-dozen projects. She probably knows as much as I do about what production companies need and what resources are available.''

"I suppose," he conceded with obvious reluctance. "So when can we expect you?''

"Next week,'' she blurted, figuring it was better to get the bad news over with in a hurry.

"No wonder you're so anxious to tout Jeannette's virtues,'' he remarked dryly. "So what's the story? Have you had major surgery over the weekend? Did you wrap your car around a tree?''

Molly noted he asked the questions with more sarcasm than concern. "Actually, Michael's uncle's boat blew up with Michael on board,'' she retorted casually.

"Yeah, right.''

"It did. Don't you ever read those papers

that stack up on your desk? Try today's front page. I'm sure Ted Ryan has a full account."

She heard the rustle of paper, then Vince's "Holy shit!"

"So, do I get the week off?"

"Is O'Hara okay?"

"Yes, but as you can tell from the commotion in the background, all is not well with the family. His uncle is missing." She held the phone out for Vince's benefit, allowing him to pick up on the upper decibels of hysteria. Satisfied that her point was made, she asked, "Get the picture?"

"Okay. O'Hara's family is noticeably distraught," he conceded. "Has something changed? Are you about to marry into this family?"

Did middle-of-the-night fantasies count? Probably not. "No," she admitted.

"Then what does this have to do with you, besides the obvious, of course, that you can't keep your nose out of trouble?"

"Let me explain the concept," she said very slowly. "Michael has stuck by me during bad times. He has been a good friend."

She ignored Vince's sarcastic *hrrmph* and plowed on. "It's my turn to return the favor. Besides, it's about time you gave Jeannette a break. The only way you'll do that is if I take off on an unscheduled vacation and she has to handle my appointments."

"Maybe I'll find out she's even better than you. Then where will you be?"

"Sitting in clover with a work load that's the size it's supposed to be," she retorted. "So what's it going to be? Do I get the time off?"

"If I say no, what will you do?"

"Take off anyway, which means you'd probably have to fire me and then hunt for a replacement. Could take weeks, maybe even months if I appeal the firing." She obviously had picked up some negotiating skills while watching Michael go at it with Public Safety Director Lucas Petty earlier at the hospital. She had an advantage, though. Vince Gates was a pushover compared to Petty. He was also pragmatic. He wanted to be on a golf course, not fighting her in some personnel dispute. Granting an unscheduled week of leave was the pragmatic answer. She waited for him to figure that out. It didn't take long.

"Okay, fine," he said grudgingly. "As long as you'll check in once a day in case there are any emergencies, I'll okay the leave. Don't get any ideas about next week, though."

Molly didn't even want to think about what would happen if they didn't find Tío Miguel long before that. "Thanks, Vince. I owe you one." It was not a balance of power she adored, but just this once there was no way around it.

When she'd hung up, she skirted the gathering of women and went to Michael's side. She found him in the midst of a quieter but no less emotional exchange between him, his uncle, and the other men from the neighborhood.

"I tell Miguel again and again that all of the plotting and scheming is no good," Tío Pedro said. "If the Bay of Pigs failed, what can one old man do?"

Molly knew a mention of the Bay of Pigs would stir the wrath of those who felt the United States had betrayed them, leaving a brigade of commandos to fight alone in a losing attack on Cuba. As expected there were immediate, passionate comments about the Cuban heroes of that 1961 attempt to reclaim their homeland and the Democratic politicians who had abandoned them. Only recently had she come to understand that more than anything else that moment in history had been responsible for turning the exile community into such passionate Republicans. Likewise, they had turned conservative because the more liberal Democrats frequently advocated a softer line with Castro.

When the reminiscences about the Bay of Pigs had run their course, Michael brought the conversation back to Miguel and the present. "Then he was still involved with that organization of the revolution or whatever it's called?" he asked.

"Two, three nights a week he sat with them over coffee at this place or that, always moving as if Castro's spies were following them," Pedro said with an air of disbelief. "Saturdays he would wear these military fatigues and go to the Everglades. When I ask him for what, he tells me they are training for the revolution."

"Didn't he read the damned newspapers?" Michael said. "The Cuban soldiers are shooting down even those who go ashore in an attempt to rescue relatives. How could he think of going back?"

His uncle sighed. "He was heartsick," Tío Pedro said. "He could not accept that the Cuba he left behind is no more. He dreamed of *café Cubano* and the white sand of Varadero beach. He saw Havana as it was when the wealthy, even from this country, came for the night life. He saw those who plotted these crazy missions as heroes of the next revolution."

"The leader is still Orestes León Paredes?" Michael asked.

"Leader?" Pedro said with derision. "What kind of leader would play on the emotions of a bunch of old men? You do not see men of your generation joining the ranks of his organization, do you? No, it is only men like Miguel, whose souls live in torment for what was."

Michael, usually so stoic and controlled, regarded his uncle with impatience. "He has been in America for more than thirty years. Why is he still clinging to the past?"

"Because he is Cuban," Pedro replied as the old men surrounding him nodded in solemn agreement. "As are you and I and your mother and your aunts. We are exiles, not Americans. We have been blessed by this country, but it is not ours. We left ours not by choice, but from necessity."

"Over thirty years," Michael repeated angrily.

"A lifetime would not change the truth," Pedro said with passion. "I might not believe that it is up to those of us here to force the changes that will make Cuba free again, but in my heart I am always Cuban."

Molly listened to the exchange with the amazement of an Anglo who had wondered time and again at the exiles' refusal to assimilate American ways. "When Castro is gone, will you go back?" she asked.

"On the first flight," Pedro said with feeling. "And yet I know it will not be the same. Perhaps I won't want to stay, but to see my homeland again? Like Miguel, I dream of it. There are cousins there I haven't seen in all these years. My brothers are there and nieces and nephews." His eyes took on a dreamy, faraway expression. "The breezes were cooler, the plantains sweeter, the *lechón* more tender."

"*Sí, sí,*" the others murmured. "That is so."

Only the nephews did not join in the chorus. They exchanged the jaded looks of children who have heard it all before time and time again.

"But you can no longer find a plantain or a pig to roast," Michael retorted.

"*Sí,*" Pedro said wearily, ignoring the bitterness in his nephew's voice. "It is the memories which are sweet, not the reality."

"You've never been back to visit?" Molly asked.

"Never. It is a choice I made. Not one dollar of my money will go into that man's pocket." He shrugged ruefully. "Not that I would be allowed back. I am regarded as an enemy of the people because I fought Fidel, because I spoke out as a dissident. Had I not escaped, I would have spent the last years jailed as so many others have."

"And Miguel?" Molly asked.

"He attempted to organize a coup. He was jailed, but made a daring escape. He was shot and left for dead. Another of the guerrillas rescued him and smuggled him aboard a boat that crossed the straits that same night. He arrived in Key West one month after my own arrival. I brought Elena with me. It was nearly a year before Pilar was able to join him. And many years after that before Michael's mother came. As the youngest of the sisters, Rosa was reluctant to leave her mother. She came only after Paolina Huerta died."

"But she sent Michael," Molly said. Michael had once told Molly of the terror of his first days in a new country, sent to live with relatives he barely remembered without the mother he adored. He had been five years old, a baby, when he left Cuba aboard one of the famed Pedro Pan freedom flights. His aching sense of being abandoned had remained with him for years. Only after they were reunited did he begin to understand that his mother had sent him away out of love.

As if all of this rhapsodic talk of a land he'd all but forgotten irritated him, Michael stood up abruptly and crossed the room to his aunt's side. Tía Pilar clasped his hand in hers and regarded him with a tear-streaked face. "Find him," she pleaded.

"I will," he promised.

His mother again stood on tiptoe and kissed him on both cheeks. "Do not take chances."

"I cannot do my job without taking chances," he told her, though a smile seemed to tug at his mouth at the start of an apparently familiar argument.

"And I cannot be a mother without warning you not to," she replied.

She walked with him back to Molly. "Thank you for coming," she said, her English precise and still reflecting her uneasiness with her second language.

"I'll be praying for Tío Miguel's safe return," Molly told her. "Please tell Tía Pilar that."

"She will be grateful. We all will."

Outside the tiny pink stucco house with its neat white trim, the street was quiet. Bright splashes of fuchsia and purple Bougainvillaea gave the simple homes a needed touch of jaunty color. Only blocks away on *Calle Ocho,* Southwest Eighth Street, the Little Havana restaurants would be opening their doors for midday meals of grilled Cuban sandwiches, chunks of pork, black beans and rice, *arroz con pollo* and sweet, fried plantains. The sidewalk stands selling *café Cubano* would already be doing a brisk business. Only Tío Pedro's restaurant would remain closed because of the family emergency.

"I'd like to make another stop before I take you home," Michael said. "Do you mind?"

"Absolutely not."

"Will Brian be okay?" he asked as an after-thought. Suddenly his expression turned worried. "Good Lord, Molly, I haven't even thought about him. Where is he?"

"He's okay. He's with his father. I called Hal from Sundays last night and asked him to keep Brian a few more days."

Michael regarded her with surprise. "You don't usually give your ex-husband that kind of concession."

She returned his gaze evenly. "I wanted to be free to help you and your family, if you'll let me. Brian will be fine with his dad for a few days. And I called Vince from your aunt's," she said. "I'm taking the week off."

She saw the trouble brewing in Michael's expressive eyes and sought to forestall it. "This isn't open for debate."

He hesitated, then finally slid his mirrored sunglasses into place and turned his attention back to the road. "Nobody's arguing, *amiga.*"

Molly was wise enough not to reach for the ever-present calendar in her purse to note the date on which macho detective Michael O'Hara finally behaved in a perfectly reasonable manner.

CHAPTER
SIX

The old men playing dominoes in Máximo Gómez Park on the corner of *Calle Ocho* and Fifteenth Avenue barely glanced up when Michael and Molly approached with the thimble-size paper cups of potent, sweet *café Cubano* they'd bought across the street. Molly watched as the tiles clicked with the precision of years of play. She listened intently to the rapid-fire Spanish to see if she could detect whether the morning's topic of conversation was the bombing of Miguel García's boat or the more general and constant theme of Castro's imminent downfall.

A portable radio blared the latest news from the most vitriolic of the Spanish-language stations. Molly recognized the histrionics of Luis Díaz-Nuñez. She couldn't interpret half of what he said. This wasn't proper, clearly enunciated

Castilian Spanish. Rather, it all ran together in a way that only someone with a trained ear could separate into distinct words. Occasionally she was able to distinguish a name or an organization, but in general she caught only the fact that whatever he was reporting made him angry and probably ought to make anyone who wasn't a traitor to the exile cause angry as well. Unfortunately for the newscaster, on this particular morning with this particular group of men, the outcome of their dominoes games took precedence over politics. Aside from an occasional halfhearted murmur of agreement, their attention was focused elsewhere.

The palm trees provided almost no breeze to stir the muggy, midsummer air. The red-tiled roofs over the tables offered minimal shade. Heat radiated from the sidewalk in shimmering waves. The aroma of cigar smoke from thick, handmade Cuban cigars made in nearby factories swirled around them. In moments their clothes were sticking to them. Still Michael stood patiently watching the play and sipping his coffee, his expression enigmatic.

Eventually, when the game he was observing most closely concluded amid cheers and back-slapping, he nodded to one of the players. "Señor López?"

Eyes the color of walnuts squinted at Michael through thick lenses. The wiry old man, his hands gnarled, his shoulders bent, finally nodded. "*Sí.* I am José López."

Michael explained in Spanish that he was Miguel García's nephew. Several men, dressed in their khaki shorts and *guayaberas,* or jeans and plain white T-shirts, backed away, looking thoroughly uneasy, as if they expected a gunfight to break out Western style. Only Señor López seemed pleased by the introduction.

"Sit," he said, gesturing to a place that was immediately vacated by his opponent in the hotly contested game of dominoes. He glanced distrustfully at Molly and waited until Michael explained who she was.

"You are wondering if I know what has happened to your uncle," he said finally, using his halting English for Molly's benefit.

Michael nodded.

"I spoke to your family last night to tell them of my concern."

"Last night? You had heard the news last night?" Michael asked skeptically. "I cannot imagine that my uncle's disappearance was on an evening newscast. One old man lost at sea for a few hours? What is the news?"

"Word travels quickly among friends. I knew of Miguel's disappearance by nightfall. Only this morning did I learn of the explosion."

"And how did you learn of that? Also from friends?"

"No, from the radio. I have heard nothing

except what was on the *noticias,* the news reports. Díaz-Nuñez has talked of little except the explosion this morning."

"And has he offered an explanation?"

"Nothing."

"He is not calling my uncle a hero?"

Señor López began to look faintly uneasy. "No, those were not his words."

"A traitor, then?"

The old man's gaze sharpened. "Why would you say such a thing?"

"It is possible, is it not? If one does not support the cause wholeheartedly, if one perhaps makes a mistake in trusting the wrong people, then there are those who would be quick to label this person a traitor. We have seen this with something as simple as the condemnation of a singer who had dared to perform in Cuba, *sí*?"

"*Es posible,* yes," Señor López admitted. "But you are speaking of your uncle. I ask again, why would you say such things?"

"Tell me about him," Michael suggested. "As you know him."

"*No comprendo.*"

"I know that you were boyhood friends in Havana. I know that he considers José López to be like a brother. I also know that you used to go with him to meetings of the Organization of the Revolution. He told me that."

A stream of Spanish greeted Michael's statement, then in English, "He should not have said that. That is Miguel's problem. He does not know how to be discreet.''

"You do not take pride in your membership?''

"That is not the point. Obviously you comprehend that no better than Miguel.''

If Michael was irritated by the criticism, Molly couldn't tell it. He was displaying far more patience with this irritable old man he ever displayed in an interrogation or even with Molly. Clearly, he expected to wheedle something important from Señor López, but Molly couldn't help wondering how long his restraint would last.

"Would that problem have caused him difficulty with Paredes?" he asked bluntly.

Molly watched Señor López's eyes at the mention of Paredes. They betrayed nothing.

He shrugged and conceded, "It is necessary to know the value of silence within a group such as ours.''

"Where can I find Paredes?''

This time there was no mistaking the flicker of unease in his eyes. López avoided Michael's gaze. "I cannot say.''

Michael's hands clenched and Molly guessed that his patience was at an end. He looked as if he wanted badly to reach across to shake the old man.

"Someone put a bomb on my uncle's boat yesterday," he said softly, though there was no mistaking his carefully contained fury. "I want to know who and I want to know why. I believe Paredes can provide the information I need."

The old man's expression shut down completely. He struggled up, and Molly realized with a sense of shock that one leg was missing below the knee. His pant leg was folded up and sewn together. She wondered when and under what circumstances his injury had occurred.

As he balanced himself carefully, one of his friends handed him a pair of crutches. "I must be going now," he said. "My daughter will be expecting me."

"You do not care what has happened to your old friend?" Michael snapped at him. "He could be dead and it does not matter to you?"

Tears brimmed in the old man's eyes before he could blink them away, and he sank back down on the concrete bench. *"Por favor,"* he whispered. "Do not do this. Leave me in peace."

"I will go," Michael said, his expression as hard and forbidding as Molly had ever seen it. "When you tell me how to find Paredes."

Señor López's hands trembled as he tried to stack the dominoes in a neat pile.

"Señor?" Michael prodded.

The dominoes tumbled to the table. "Tomorrow night at La Carreta." Lopez said finally, referring to a chain of Cuban family-style restaurants.

"Which one?"

"Here, on *Calle Ocho*."

"And Paredes will be there?"

"Perhaps. Perhaps not. But someone there will know how to find him."

Michael gave a curt nod of satisfaction, then rested his hand over the old man's. "Thank you."

"De nada." For nothing. No problem.

It wasn't nothing, though, Molly realized as she studied the soul-weary man across from them. José López looked as if the exchange had drained him of every last bit of energy. Worse, when she gazed into his eyes, all she saw was fear.

As she and Michael walked back to his car, she said to him, "He was afraid. Was it because you're a policeman?"

Michael shook his head. "I believe he is afraid that whatever happened to my uncle could happen to him."

• • •

Michael fell sound asleep en route to his recently acquired townhouse in Kendall. Not even the caffeine in several cups of Cuban coffee could combat the exhaustion of the past twenty-four hours or so. The fact that he was not awake to argue was probably the only reason Molly was actually able to get him to go home. Awake he would have been insisting on going to assist in the rescue flights that had been taking off all morning from Tamiami Airport in search of his uncle and any other misguided rafters who might be lost on the treacherous seas.

He groaned when she gently shook him awake to go inside. "Where are we?"

"Your place."

He yawned and climbed out of the car, leading the way inside the neat cream-colored structure with its red-tiled roof. Inside the air-conditioning blasted, creating an almost Arctic chill.

"I'll take a quick shower and then go out to the airport," he said, his voice still groggy with sleep. "Why don't you get some rest?"

Molly lost patience. "Michael, if you keep this up, you're going to collapse. Then what will your family do? Sleep for a couple of hours at least. Then you can go to the airport and wait for the rescue flights to come in."

"I should be on board one of them."

"Taking the place of someone whose eyes are alert?"

He sighed then. "Okay, you have a point."

"Remind me to mark the occasion."

"Careful, *amiga*, or I will find a way to silence that tart tongue of yours."

She grinned at him. "I'd be worried, if you weren't asleep on your feet."

"There are some things a man can always find the energy to do."

Molly wanted very much to suggest he prove it, but concluded reluctantly that this was definitely not the time. "I'll remind you of that one of these days. Go, get some rest. I'll wake you in a couple of hours."

"You need rest, too, *amiga*."

"I need to make a couple of calls, then I'll lie down right here on the sofa." She thought it was an amazingly noble suggestion considering where she'd rather be.

To her surprise, he shook his head. "I want you beside me," he said, though there was less amorous intent in his words than a sort of lost desolation. "Please."

Deeply touched, her pulse hammering, Molly nodded. "I'll be there as soon as I check on Brian."

The call to Hal to exact his promise to keep Brian until the crisis with Tío Miguel was resolved took far less time than she'd anticipated, mostly because for once Hal didn't argue with her. In a resigned, only faintly aggrieved tone, he simply agreed.

"I hope everything turns out okay," he said. "I saw the story this morning."

"Did Brian see it?" she asked worriedly.

"No, I didn't even open the paper until I got to the office. O'Hara's okay?"

"Exhausted, but okay. I'll talk to you soon."

"Molly?"

"Yes?"

"I know you don't want to hear this from me, but be careful. You've seen the extremes some of these people will go to to make a point."

Molly thought of the radio newscaster years before whose leg had been blown off by a car bomb. She recalled the bombs detonated to make a point about a collection of artworks that had contained paintings by artists still living in Cuba. She thought of the campaign of death threats and harassment conducted against the city's newspaper. And then she remembered the fiery explosion just after midnight on the bay and shuddered.

"Yes, I've seen it, all too recently. Tell Brian I love him, okay? I'll call him as soon as I can. Please reassure him that Michael is fine."

When she'd finished talking to her ex-husband, she made one more call, this one to Ted Ryan at the morning paper.

"Molly, this is a switch, you calling me."

She knew she was taking a risk involving the reporter. Michael would be furious if he found out. But her own sources in the Cuban community tended to be middle-class exiles, who maintained an allegiance to their homeland but kept themselves far removed from the politics of terrorism—at least officially. The paper, however, had sources in this exile underground that she would never be able to tap without an introduction. Even Michael would be regarded with suspicion. Señor López's distrustful, frightened reaction had proved that, as had the nervousness of those who'd witnessed the exchange in the park.

"I need your help," she told Ted.

"Anything," he said at once. "You know that."

"I want everything you have in the files about Orestes León Paredes and that organization he leads. Can you do that?"

"No problem. I'll get printouts for you this afternoon. What's he have to do with the bombing?"

"That's what I'm trying to find out. Can you ask around over there and find out where he lives or where he has his headquarters?"

"Sure. Is there a number where I can call you back?"

"I'll call you later." She glanced at the clock on the kitchen wall. It was already after noon. "How about three o'clock?"

"I'll be here."

"Thanks, Ted."

When she'd hung up, she glanced around Michael's kitchen, amazed as always at its pristine cleanliness. Not one single dirty dish sat in the sink. She knew if she looked into the dishwasher, she would find none in there either. Unlike most bachelor refrigerators, his would be well-stocked with healthy foods, all carefully wrapped. Most impressive was the restaurant-quality espresso machine on the counter and the array of blended coffees displayed beside it. Michael did love his coffee. Hers, he claimed, was weak, sissy stuff.

The first time she had come here, only a few

weeks earlier after one of Brian's soccer games, Molly had commented on the neatness of his kitchen. Michael had merely shrugged and gone about the business of putting together a snack for Brian and his teammates with astonishing efficiency. It was, she had since concluded, the same way he approached everything in his life. He kept things precisely ordered so there was no distracting clutter to interfere with the constant mulling of clues and evidence that went on in his head.

Surprised by her own reluctance, she finally forced herself toward the steps leading to the townhouse's second-floor bedrooms. This was new terrain to her in more ways than one. She wondered if, once she had climbed those stairs, things would ever be the same between them again.

Not because of sex, she told herself. She didn't think that was what was on Michael's mind anyway. No, because of the vulnerability he had allowed her to see for the first time today. That bond of emotional intimacy was something she had craved far more than physical contact, although there was no denying that more and more lately she'd had restless nights from wanting the sexy, elusive Cuban detective to hold her in his arms.

Taking a deep breath at the partially-closed door to his room, she pushed the door open, uncertain of what to expect. Disappointment warred with amusement at what she found.

Michael was sprawled facedown across the bed, his upper body bare, a pair of colorful boxer shorts riding low on his hips, his black hair still damp from his shower.

So much for crawling into bed beside him, she thought ruefully, as she examined the odd patches of space here and there on the king-size bed. He'd taken his side of the bed in the middle. She stood for a long time, just drinking in the sight of all that leanly-muscled masculinity. The perfection had been seriously marred by the explosion. Stitched gashes and bright bruises were stark testimony to his close call.

Sighing, she finally plucked up the alarm clock from beside the bed, quietly closed the door, and crept back downstairs for her own desperately needed nap.

She set the clock for two thirty. It was barely more than twenty-four hours since she and Michael had begun worrying that something had happened to Tío Miguel. It seemed like a lifetime ago, a lifetime crammed with emotional extremes.

As she curled up on Michael's oversize cream-colored sofa with its plump pillows, she realized there was no way of knowing how long it might be before either of them slept again.

CHAPTER
SEVEN

Molly was awakened not by the alarm clock, but by the sound of voices. No, not *voices*. One very loud, angry voice. Michael's.

She glanced at the clock and saw that it was just after two o'clock. Groaning, she turned off the alarm before its shrill could join the commotion from upstairs and buried her face in a pillow. She indulged in a moment's regret that it had been the clock, not the phone she had removed from his room. She felt dull and headachy, not rested at all. Michael, on the other hand, seemed to have found the energy to yell. His voice carried through the townhouse.

"What the hell do you mean, they're calling off the search? My uncle could be dying out there."

There was a brief lull, then, "Thunderstorms? Who gives a shit? I don't care if a god-damned hurricane is brewing, I want those planes to cover every square inch of water in the straits.''

Molly dragged herself off the sofa. Obviously she needed to get upstairs and explain the concept of winning friends and influencing people to Michael before he alienated the only people actually searching for his uncle.

She found him sitting on the side of his bed, clothed only in those brightly patterned boxer shorts, lines of exhaustion still etched on his face. He barely even glanced at her as she sat down next to him.

Acting instinctively, she put her hand on his bare shoulder in a gesture meant to soothe. It might not have soothed, but it definitely got his attention. Obviously, a woman's hand on his na-ked flesh was to Michael what a red cape was to a bull—the start of something. Heat flared in his eyes.

"Yeah, yeah, I understand," he muttered distractedly.

His gaze locked with Molly's. She burned under the intensity of his scrutiny. She decided that just maybe he'd gotten the wrong idea.

Or the right idea at the wrong time, to be perfectly honest about it.

He hung up, his gaze still so hot it could melt icier resolve than Molly's.

"What brings you upstairs, *amiga?*"

"The call of the wild," she replied.

He looked absolutely fascinated. A spark of purely provocative devilment lit his eyes. "Oh, really?"

"You were shouting insults at the top of your lungs. I decided drastic measures were called for to mellow you out."

"How drastic?"

She stood up and backed away from temptation. "Well, much as I'd like to stay and demonstrate, isn't it time we got back to our investigation?"

"Our investigation?"

Heady from earlier successful negotiations with the likes of Vince Gates and Hal DeWitt, she decided to test Michael's limits. "Right. We're a team. Partners. Remember?"

His gaze slid over her. "That's not what I remember. What I remember was inviting you to share my bed."

"Michael, has it occurred to you that you have picked a very odd time to decide you want to seduce me?" She actually thought it was a pretty good show of indignation coming from a woman only one heartbeat away from flinging herself into that bed with him.

He shook his head. Amusement flared in his eyes. "This is not a recent decision, *amiga.*"

"Okay, to act on it, then."

"Does that mean you're not interested in

crawling back into this nice, warm bed with me?" he inquired doubtfully. "Tell the truth."

Molly couldn't have lied if her life depended on it. It was just as well. Michael was used to detecting when people were lying through their teeth. It would have been no contest. "Yes. As a matter of fact, the idea holds a great deal of appeal," she admitted.

As he reached for her, his expression reeking of smug satisfaction, she added, "But I'm not sure I can fight these nagging images of Tía Pilar weeping for her missing husband."

Michael put his head in his hands and groaned. "You really know how to spoil a moment, don't you?"

"Better to spoil this one than deal with your regrets the rest of the day."

He shot her a rueful grin. "You have a point."

"I always do. You just rarely listen. Hand me the phone."

"What for?"

She scowled at him. "Just hand it over, please."

When she had it, she dialed Ted Ryan's number. Michael stood up, found a pair of tan slacks and a soft-beige designer shirt and pulled them on while she waited for the reporter to pick up. She studied his polished designer look enviously, then glanced down at her own wrinkled walking shorts and short-sleeved blouse, which she'd been wearing since the day before. She wondered if she'd ever get home long enough to change. She also wondered about a man who saw past the rumpled clothes and still found an attractive, desirable woman. He definitely had to be some sort of national treasure.

Ted picked up while she was still mentally enumerating more of Michael's endearing attributes. "Were you able to get that information I asked for?" she asked.

"Sure did. I've got a huge stack of printouts for you. You can pick them up anytime. I'll leave them at the information desk downstairs in case I'm not here when you stop by. As for Paredes, he lives in Westchester in some nondescript little house on a quiet street." He hesitated. "Molly, are you sure you want to get to him yourself? He maintains a pretty low profile. He won't be pleased to have you drop by, if that's what you have in mind. He's liable to greet you with an assault rifle."

"I can hardly wait," Molly muttered as she jotted down the address on the pad Michael had on the nightstand by the bed. "Thanks."

"Tell me you're not going out there alone," he insisted.

"I'm not."

"That's a relief. One last thing."

"What's that?"

"Forget where you got this information, okay?"

"It just appeared to me in a vision," she agreed.

Michael watched her intently as she hung up. "What was all that about visions? Don't tell me it was a call to the Psychic Friends Network."

Scowling at him, she held out the piece of paper. "Here you go," she said, then added with a certain pointed emphasis, "partner."

Michael looked at the address. "What's this?"

"The closely guarded home address of Orestes León Paredes."

Michael didn't waste time on astonishment or applause. His expression grim, he put on his shoulder holster, added a neatly-pressed jacket that made Molly feel more rumpled than ever, and gestured toward the bedroom door. "Let's go, *partner*."

• • •

Molly was able to persuade her new investigative partner to detour past the paper by promising him more information than he could possibly gather on his own in days of interrogations, even if he could find people who'd talk to him.

When she emerged from the paper's lobby with an armload of computer printouts, he looked downright impressed and maybe just a little worried.

"Exactly what did you have to promise Ryan to get all this?"

"First crack at any major break in the case."

"Given the way he feels about you, I'm surprised he didn't hold out for a more personal commitment."

She frowned at him. "You're the only one who thinks he has a crush on me."

"Only because you are blind to the signs."

"Why are we arguing over Ted Ryan's amorous intentions, when we should be thanking our lucky stars that he dumped all this information into our laps?"

"You have a point. You read while I drive."

Molly had barely made a dent in the material, when they neared Paredes's neighborhood.

Westchester was a community west of the Florida Turnpike, where many Cubans had eventually settled, leaving Little Havana to a more recent influx of exiles from El Salvador, Nicaragua, and Panama.

Along the Tamiami Trail, yet another designation for *Calle Ocho* or Southwest Eighth Street before it continued west to cut through the Everglades toward Naples, there were strip malls and gun shops, a bowling alley, and dozens of neat little restaurants featuring a mix of ethnic fare. One of the most popular Cuban restaurants, Lila's, with its mounds of crisp *papas fritas*—fried potatoes—atop tender *palomilla* steak, beckoned as Michael and Molly headed for their unscheduled meeting with Paredes.

Refusing to waste time for a sit-down meal,

Michael conceded only to picking up two grilled sandwiches, *media noches* as they were called by Cubans and Anglos alike. They ate the sandwiches as he made the turn off the Trail into a neighborhood of Spanish-style homes with neat lawns and climbing bougainvillaea in vivid shades of purple and fuchsia. Ornamental ironwork covered most of the windows, installed not for its intricate beauty, but to protect against crime. In this respect it was not so different from Little Havana. Here, though, the homes were slightly larger and newer.

"How'd you get the address?" he asked as he checked the numbers on the houses against the slip of paper.

Molly was amazed the question hadn't come up before now. Maybe he just hadn't had the energy to look a gift horse in the mouth. Well fed now, his naturally suspicious brain had kicked in.

"Sources," she said enigmatically.

"What sources?"

"What difference does it make?"

"I'm not sure anyone on the Metro police force could get this address, yet one lone county employee just snaps her fingers and has it. It doesn't figure."

"Oh, I'm sure some enterprising cop over there has it tucked away in his Rolodex for a rainy day."

Michael shook his head. "Just about the time

anyone pins down his location, Paredes shifts to a new spot. I suppose it's habit after years of moving his guerrilla camps around the Cuban countryside to evade Castro's soldiers. So what did you barter with this so-called source of yours to get it? Or was this just more of Ted Ryan's largesse?''

"Michael, not everything in life has a price tag.''

"Yes, *amiga,* sooner or later it does. You just haven't been asked to pay up yet.''

Molly decided nothing she was likely to say would counteract that level of ingrained cynicism. She kept her mouth clamped firmly shut.

When they finally reached the address she had been given, the house looked exactly like every other house on the block. There was nothing to distinguish it, right down to the clutter of toys on the front lawn and the rusty, aging sedan in the driveway, along with a newer, though still not brand-new, car parked behind it. Molly glanced up and down the block in amazement.

"I didn't know there were this many old cars still in existence in running order,'' she said.

"You should see the ones on the streets of Havana. I'm told those make these old clunkers look like the latest models. A lot of people have become very adept mechanics.'' As he cut off the ignition, he glanced at her, his expression suddenly serious. "*Amiga,* don't get all bent out of shape over this . . .''

"Uh-oh. What?"

"I think it might be best for you to wait in the car."

"Why?" she asked, though she was relatively certain she knew what was coming. She doubted it was because he was ashamed of her appearance.

"If Paredes is even here, he may not be willing to talk with you present," Michael explained cautiously.

"Because I'm an Anglo?"

"Worse," he admitted.

"What could be worse?"

"Because you are a woman."

"Of all the idiotic, chauvinistic attitudes," she said without much energy. As much as she hated the macho world of a certain breed of Hispanic men, it was relatively pointless to flail away at its existence. The discovery that Paredes was such a man wasn't exactly a stunning surprise.

"I don't suppose now is the time to try to mend his ways, though, is it?" she said with an air of resignation.

"Not really."

"Okay. I will wait in the car like the dutiful little woman."

"Thanks."

"No problem." As Michael stepped out of the car, she beckoned him back. "Just one thing."

He regarded her warily. "What?"

"Hand over your cellular phone."

He gave it to her with trepidation written all over his face. "You don't know anyone on the other side of the world, do you? Liza, for example," he said, referring to Molly's best friend and neighbor. "Isn't she on some trip to the rain forest again?"

"Worried about me running up your bill? As a matter of fact, Liza's in Tibet," she informed him cheerfully. "Hurry back."

With one last worried look over his shoulder, Michael walked determinedly up to Orestes León Paredes's front door and knocked. Heavy draperies slid aside a fraction while someone peered out. Then the door opened a cautious inch. She noticed Michael did not flash his badge. Whatever he said, though, got him admitted.

Molly caught a brief glimpse of a tall, olive-complexioned man, his military fatigues straining over a potbelly, right before the door slammed shut and what sounded like a seriously heavy-duty bolt slid home. It was not a comforting sound. The only thing keeping her from outright panic was the reassuring weight of that cellular phone and the knowledge that help was only three quick digits away.

CHAPTER
EIGHT

Huge, heavy black clouds began to build up to the west over the Everglades. Molly put the cellular phone on the dash as thunder rumbled through the muggy air. A jagged bolt of lightning split the sky, followed within seconds by the ear-splitting crack of thunder. The first fat drops of rain splashed against the windshield, followed instants later by a downpour so intense she could barely see the house only fifteen yards or less away. She felt cut off and isolated as she waited for Michael to return. The feelings of foreboding that had begun with the slamming of that door no longer seemed quite so absurd.

To distract herself, she tried to read more printouts. Gradually she began to put together an impression of Orestes León Paredes. He was a man who came from great wealth in Cuba, only to have his property taken over by the government. Angered by the loss and young enough to take his ideals to the streets, he had publicly opposed Castro, organizing a band of guerrillas known for the daring and violence of their attacks. He had brought the same attitudes and tenacity with him when he escaped to Miami.

He had participated in the CIA-planned Bay of Pigs invasion, meant to spark an uprising of the Cuban people. It had failed dramatically. But once again the remarkable Paredes luck had held. He had neither died nor been taken prisoner. He had just added to his mystique.

He had also realized during that abysmal failure that any overthrow of Castro was in the hands of those who believed as passionately as he did. They could not count on Washington for the help they needed.

Over the years since then, he had surrounded himself with a veritable army of commandos anxious for their chance to provide the spark that would ignite a revolution. Molly wondered if even now Miguel was in Cuba fanning such flames at Paredes's instigation.

Little was written about his personal life, but judging from the toys scattered on his lawn, he had children or grandchildren. She wondered if he was instilling the same anger and fighting spirit in them.

Eventually she glanced up from the pages. There was still no sign of Michael. "Come on, dammit," she whispered, her gaze pinned on the shadowy outline of the house. She checked her watch again. It was nearly four o'clock. Michael had been inside for little more than a half hour. It just seemed like longer. She would give him another fifteen minutes before she gave in to panic and called 911.

She kept her gaze fixed on the house, unwilling to look away even to read more of the articles Ted had provided. The only time her gaze strayed was when she glanced at her watch. The second hand was moving at a snail's pace. *Tick. Tick. Tick.* She drew in deep gulps of breath with every tick. At this rate, she'd hyperventilate and the 911 call would be for paramedics for her. *Tick. Tick.*

Another streak of lightning split the nearby sky, followed almost at once by the sharp crack of thunder. It was so close that it seemed to rock the car like a child's toy in a giant's grip.

Finally the sheets of rain dwindled into occasional fat drops again. The black clouds rolled on toward the east, leaving blue skies and bright sunshine, with steam rising from the pavement. The rumbling of the thunder receded into the distance. It was almost as if the storm had never happened.

Unfortunately, Molly's pulse still wouldn't settle back into an easy rhythm. The fifteen minutes were past. Michael had been inside for nearly an hour.

Okay, she thought. So it had been an hour. He and Paredes had a lot to talk about. He wouldn't appreciate her calling for backup if everything inside was perfectly fine. The only way to determine that for sure would be to get a glimpse inside that house. How she was going to do that was a problem.

The front windows were covered by those heavy drapes. There was a fence around the side and back yards. There was, however, a gate on the east side of the house, right at the end of the driveway. She wondered if she could get to that gate without being seen, especially with the passenger door of the car in full view of the house.

Oh, well, nothing beats a try but a failure, she recalled her mother telling her on some occasion when her usually intrepid spirit had failed her. She slid to the driver's side and carefully opened the door. Right before she stepped out, she grabbed the phone and tucked it into the waistband of her walking shorts. Okay, it didn't exactly imply the same level of protection as a gun, but it was all she had.

The air was even steamier after the brief storm. It was sort of like breathing through a damp cloth. Her clothes stuck to her skin. Staying low, she moved from beside Michael's car to the far side of the cars parked in the driveway. With her gaze locked on the front windows of the house, she inched her way toward that gate.

She had one hand on the opened latch and

one foot inside when all hell broke loose. Two snapping, snarling pit bulls rounded a corner of the house. With her heart slamming against her chest, Molly rammed the gate closed and prayed the latch would hold against the weight of their frantic bodies being thrown against it again and again as they tried to get to her.

The front door of the house opened and Michael and the man she'd seen earlier came tearing outside. At the sight of Molly standing on the far side of his car, bent over and trying to catch her breath, Michael slowed.

"Going for a walk?" he inquired dryly as the other man sharply ordered the dogs to the back of the house. They slunk away.

Molly couldn't seem to stop shaking. Still she tried to bluster her way out of the incriminating mess. "Yes. It was hot in the car after the storm. I thought I'd get some air."

Michael looked as if he didn't believe that any more than he believed pigs flew. Obviously, though, he didn't intend to call her on it in front of his host. She'd probably pay for that bit of discretion later.

The man gestured toward Molly. "She is with you?" he asked Michael.

"Yes."

"And you allowed her to remain outside in this heat? I am surprised at you," he said, coming forward. He took Molly's hand and bowed over it in a courtly gesture at odds with the military attire and suburban setting. "Señorita, I am Paredes."

Molly gazed into dark, almost black eyes that reflected intelligence and an innate wariness that belied the polite greeting. He looked to be in his late fifties, his face weathered by time and sun, his dark brown hair streaked with gray. Despite the potbelly, he appeared to be in decent shape. The muscles in his forearms were well defined. Anyone misjudging his strength would no doubt be in for a rude awakening.

"Molly DeWitt," she said, trying not to recoil from his powerful grip or his intense, distrustful scrutiny. "I'm sorry for disturbing your meeting. I hadn't realized you had dogs."

"Their purpose is better served if they take people by surprise," he said dryly.

"I'm sure."

"You would like to join us, perhaps?"

Michael gave an almost imperceptible shake of his head. "Our meeting is concluded, wouldn't you say, Señor Paredes?"

A flash of anger darkened the older man's eyes, but was hurriedly replaced by a jovial expression. He bowed again to Molly. "Perhaps another time, señorita. I will look forward to it."

"Perhaps." There was something in his voice that made Molly feel as if he'd just made an indecent pass at her, though his actual words and expression couldn't have been more innocuous. She gathered Michael had heard that sleazy note as well since he looked as if he wanted to throttle the man.

Molly didn't relax until they were out of the neighborhood. Michael's stony silence didn't help.

"What did he tell you?" she asked finally.

"You mean besides the forty-five-minute recruitment pitch?"

"He wants you to join the organization?"

"He suggested I would be a traitor to my heritage if I did not."

"Did you sign up?"

Michael scowled at her. "No, *amiga*, I did not sign up. His is a fool's mission."

"He obviously does not feel that way. Nor did Tío Miguel."

"More's the pity."

"Did he tell you anything about your uncle?"

"He praised him as a valiant hero. He said he cannot imagine what has become of him, that there was no secret invasion planned for Sunday. He denied that anyone connected with his organization might have wanted to harm Miguel."

"How does he explain the disappearance?"

"A mishap at sea."

Molly regarded him incredulously. "And the bomb?"

"It is beyond his comprehension," Michael said dryly.

"I'll bet. He's a cold, calculating man."

"Except when he looks at you. Obviously, you stir the hot-blooded passion in him."

Molly glanced at his set jaw. "Surely you are not jealous of him?"

"Men like Paredes can have a certain charismatic charm, *amiga*. That is how they command so many followers."

She shrugged. "I don't see it."

"Good."

● ● ●

When Molly and Michael arrived at Tamiami Airport after an amazingly quick trip down the Turnpike given the rush-hour conditions, they found not just the pilots who had been searching the waters between Cuba and the Florida Keys that day, but a growing crowd of Cubans, U.S. Immigration officials, and reporters.

Huddled in front of a half-dozen microphones inside a hangar were two young teenage boys who seemed stunned by all the attention. In low voices, they told of their ordeal at sea. Their stories were repeated in English by a translator who stood beside them.

"For months we scoured the countryside in search of old inner tubes and scraps of lumber," Ricardo Rodríguez said. He was painfully thin, his skin parched by the sun. The man who'd introduced him had given his age as sixteen. "It was our dream to come to America, where there is food and work."

"How long were you at sea?" a reporter asked.

"Six days we fought the currents. The waves washed our water and food overboard on the fourth day," the same boy said.

"There were sharks," his companion, Tony Suárez, added. He appeared to be shy, or perhaps he was just terribly shaken. His voice was barely above a whisper. "They came to our raft. I thought for sure we were going to die. Our friend Tomás . . ." His voice faltered.

"There was another boy with you?" a reporter asked, his voice unexpectedly thick with emotion.

The two nodded. "He went crazy. The sun. No water. It made him *loco*. He dove into the sea. He said he wished to swim home."

"When was that?"

"An hour, perhaps two, before we heard the plane," the boy said, his own voice quivering. "If only he had waited . . ."

"Where were they when you found them?" a reporter asked the two pilots standing behind the boys.

"Miles from land. Perhaps in another day or two, perhaps longer, they might have drifted ashore who knows where along the coast. By then, without water or food . . ." He shrugged. "Their fate would have been no better than their friend's."

Molly glanced at Michael and saw that the

color had drained out of his face. Because of those damnable sunglasses, she couldn't gauge the turmoil in his expressive eyes. His tightened jaw, however, was telling enough. She wasn't certain whether his reaction of horror had to do with these courageous boys who had survived thanks to some whim of timing and luck that had brought them into the view of the rescuers or whether he was thinking of his uncle, who might still be drifting on the same treacherous seas.

When the press conference ended a short time later, Michael went to one of the Immigration officials and introduced himself.

"How many are there like this?"

"You mean teens arriving alone?"

Michael nodded.

"I'd say one in eight of every new arrival is between fourteen and twenty-one," he said matter-of-factly. Clearly such statistics were commonplace to him, but Molly was stunned.

"Dear heaven," she whispered.

Michael glanced at the two boys. "What will happen to them now? Do they have relatives here who will take them in?"

"They claim to have an uncle here, but we haven't been able to locate him. They will go to a halfway house designed for the teenagers who have come alone from Cuba. It is already overcrowded, but they'll make room. The boys will be able to stay there until they acclimate and find work."

He regarded Michael soberly. "It won't be easy for them. They come here so filled with hope, and then they discover that even in Miami, where the Cuban culture has been maintained in so many ways, they are homesick. Worse, they're surrounded by so many material goods and foods for the first time in their lives, and they don't have the money to buy what they want. In some ways, for many of them that is worse than not having it available in the first place."

"So they start to steal," Michael guessed, his gaze pinned on the two youngsters who were being treated as heroes by the gathering of Cubans who'd heard of the rescue. Their presence confirmed what José López had explained earlier, word of mouth in the exile community was swift.

"Or they try to go back to Cuba," the Immigration officer told them.

His expression bleak, Michael walked to the front of the hangar. He introduced himself to the teenagers, who were beginning to show signs of exhaustion. Molly stood beside him as he spoke to them quietly in Spanish. He took his business cards from his pocket and gave one to each of them. As he talked, their eyes never left his face as if they were experiencing the same intangible bond that had drawn Michael to them. They nodded solemnly as they listened.

At last he grinned and shook their hands. Shy smiles broke across their thin faces, lighting their eyes. Then Michael turned abruptly and walked out of the hangar.

When Molly found him, he was standing in the shade of an overhang, the tarmac around them radiating the late-afternoon heat. His expression looked haunted.

"Michael?"

He reached for her hand and pulled her close, resting his chin atop her head. "I can't imagine it," he said. "I can't imagine what it would be like to be so desperate at their age that I would risk crossing the sea on a bunch of goddamned tires and pieces of lumber."

"You told them you'd help them, didn't you?"

"I will do what I can. Tío Pedro is always looking for willing workers at the restaurant. And I can see that they have clothing and a few of the things that boys need to feel as if they belong."

"If what the man from Immigration said is true, there are many more like them. You can't help them all."

He shrugged. "Perhaps not, but I can do something for these two. I can do it in honor of Tío Miguel. It is what he would want."

CHAPTER
NINE

"Aside from the two boys, we saw only an empty raft today," pilot Ricardo Bienes told Michael when they went back inside the hangar where the jubilant crowd was still celebrating the rescue of the two teenagers. "I am sorry."

"You are certain the raft was not my uncle's?"

Bienes gestured toward the front of the room, where the makeshift contraption was on display. Molly shuddered as she took a really good look at it for the first time. Even though the boys had described their own similar raft, the sight of those inner tubes and scraps of lumber made her heart ache at the desperation involved in assembling such a craft. It looked pitifully inadequate for crossing any water wider or rougher than a pond. Obviously Michael hadn't even glanced at it or he would never have asked the question.

"As you can see for yourself, it was crudely made," Bienes said. "It is definitely not the sort your uncle would have had on board his boat. It would appear that whoever was aboard this flimsy vessel perished at sea, unless they were rescued earlier by a passing boat."

"How often does that happen?" Molly asked as Michael continued to study the raft with obvious dismay.

"Often enough. Even the *Britannia,* the Queen of England's yacht, has picked up a Cuban rafter trying to reach America. Freighters, cruise ships, fishing boats . . ." The pilot shrugged. "Most anyone will rescue those fleeing Cuba, if they see them. Who could leave a human being aboard a raft such as this on the open seas?"

Once assured that there could be no mistaking this particular raft for his uncle's, Michael lost interest in it and the more general statistics. "You will look for my uncle again tomorrow?"

Bienes shook his head. "I understand your situation, but that is not possible. We are volunteers, my friend. Tomorrow we must work. We go out only three days a week, taking turns so that jobs are not jeopardized."

"Please," Michael implored.

The stark emotion on his face and in his

voice was raw and vulnerable. It was a dramatic contrast to his usual stoic silences and unreadable expressions. Molly wanted to reach out to him, but knew he wouldn't thank her for the gesture. He'd view it as an acknowledgment of a weakness.

"I will make a donation for your time, something to pay for fuel for other flights," he added.

Before Bienes could respond, a second pilot, Jorge Martinez, joined them. He gave Michael's shoulder the reassuring squeeze that Molly hadn't dared.

"Do not worry. We will make arrangements to have someone in the air tomorrow," he promised. At Bienes's surprised expression, he added, "Miguel and Pilar were very good to me and my family when we arrived here. I owe this to him."

"I could take one plane up myself," Michael suggested. "I'm licensed."

"That is not necessary," Martinez said. "Others will volunteer, I am sure," he added with a pointed look at his colleague.

Bienes sighed. "I suppose one more day of missed work will not matter."

"Who would fire you, eh?" Martinez asked him. "You are your own boss."

"And when I am not there, nothing gets done," Bienes countered with a rueful expression. "But under these circumstances, I suppose that does not matter."

"God will reward you for your good deeds," Martinez assured him.

"Perhaps some of my clients will pay their bills, then, yes?"

"For that you need a collection agency, not divine intervention."

"What do you do?" Molly asked Bienes.

"I am an attorney."

"A very well-paid attorney," Martinez added. "Do not let him stir your pity, señorita. He will not wind up in the poorhouse because of one extra day off. Besides, he loves any excuse to fly that fancy new plane of his, a plane paid for by the very clients he would have you believe are deadbeats."

"I think what you're doing is wonderful," Molly told both men. "Not many would dedicate themselves to such exhausting searches, especially when the results are so often tragic."

"But there are days like today," Martinez reminded her, "when our efforts are rewarded. It is these moments we cherish. It is what we owe to those who remained behind in Cuba and now can fight no more, to those who desperately seek to escape the suffering."

"When did you come to the United States?" Molly asked him. "During the freedom flights in the sixties?"

"No. Much later. It was Miguel who rescued us." He glanced at Michael. "You did not know that, did you, my friend? Your uncle brought his fishing boat to Mariel in the days of the boatlift in 1980. He brought us here at the request of my wife's brother. He took nothing for his time and trouble. As I said before, my family owes Miguel García.''

From the distance of a college campus, Molly had read hundreds of similar stories at the tumultuous time of the boat lift. Every available seaworthy vessel and some, perhaps, that were not, made trip after trip to Mariel to bring back those who wished to flee the island, along with those Castro himself deemed unfit to stay, including prisoners and the mentally ill. One hundred twenty-five thousand in all.

But now, for the first time, looking into Jorge Martinez's eyes and seeing the gratitude reflected there, she understood the powerful ties binding those who had gone through that particular Cuban exile experience. He clasped Michael's hand.

''We will do this search for Miguel,'' he said. ''You will be more valuable here, conducting your investigation.'' He patted his pocket. ''I have your beeper number. You will know the minute we find him.''

''And if you don't?''

''Trust me, my friend. If Miguel is on the seas, we will find him. I make that promise to you.''

• • •

When they left the airstrip in southwest Dade, Molly debated insisting on going home to Key Biscayne to shower and change, but decided that would give Michael a perfect excuse for dumping her there. Instead, she persuaded him to make a quick stop at Dadeland Mall, where she bought two pairs of lightweight slacks, a couple of T-shirts, and a few other necessities. She was back at the car, where Michael was making phone calls, in the promised twenty minutes.

"Any news?" she asked.

"Nothing. I talked to Tío Pedro and he said there was nothing on the national news or the local news about any kind of guerrilla excursion into Cuba. If that's where Miguel was headed, he arrived safely and without being detected or he is still adrift in those damnable straits." He regarded Molly with a bleak expression. "Who knows how long he can survive out there."

"Those boys were at sea for six days, two of those days without water or food," Molly reminded him.

"But as you said, they are boys. Miguel is an old man. And I saw for myself that his provisions remained on his boat. More and more I am convinced he was forced onto that raft. Perhaps he was intentionally cast adrift to die."

"But why?"

"I don't know," he admitted, his voice tight

with frustration. "But I would bet my life that Paredes is the key."

"Maybe Felipe and Ken will have some answers," Molly said as they turned into Michael's townhouse development.

Sure enough, both policemen were sitting on the front steps of Michael's condominium. For the first time Molly had a chance to study them more closely. In the chaos of the previous night she had gathered only vague impressions.

Ken Marshall looked to be in his late thirties, though there was already a lot of gray in his curly brown hair. His hazel eyes were unflinching. She had seen for herself that it was a quietly intelligent gaze that could be both compassionate and unnerving. Perhaps that intensity was what made him such an outstanding evidence technician. She could believe that absolutely nothing got past him.

Felipe Domínguez was his opposite in many ways. Short, while Ken was tall, mischievous, while Ken was serious, Felipe had the square build of a boxer and the attitude of a street fighter.

At the moment they were engaged in an obviously intense discussion. Their expressions turned even more sober at the sight of Michael. Inside, over the promised pizza and beer, they offered little new information.

"We have bits and pieces from the boat," Ken said. "But nothing at all of the bomb." He glanced at Molly. "Felipe and I have been trying to remember any details from that quick look we took. We're coming up blank. Can you recall anything at all about what you saw?"

"I heard it. I didn't get a good look at it. It sounded like a standard wind-up clock."

Ken's gaze narrowed. "Why wind-up?"

"The ticking," she said immediately and without a doubt. "When I was a kid, I had an inexpensive clock that made that same sound by my bed. Electric and digital clocks make a quieter sound, if they make any noise at all."

"She's right," Felipe said. "It sounded like the clock I picked up at the drugstore when our electric clock died a few weeks ago." He paused a minute, then added, "Like that clock the crocodile swallowed in *Peter Pan*."

"Terrific," Michael muttered. "The timing device could have been bought in any one of hundreds of chain drugstores around town. That really narrows things way the hell down."

Ken regarded him sympathetically. "Hey, pal, I know you're frustrated, but what Molly said comes as no surprise. For all the talk of training exercises and stuff, we're not talking a high-tech military operation here. We're probably not even talking about professional international terrorists. I'd guess this was somebody with an ax to grind and one of those primitive but effective how-to-stir-up-insurrection manuals. Back when people were bombing the hell out of the homes and businesses of anyone they thought was soft on Fidel, they weren't using plastique and that fancy garbage. What they came up with was crude, but it did the job."

"Which brings us back to Paredes and people like him," Michael said, glancing at Felipe. "What did you learn on the streets?"

"I got a lot of shock, a lot of outrage, and not one single lead. When I mentioned Paredes and his organization, a few people looked very nervous but denied knowing of any connection."

"Were they lying?" Michael asked.

Felipe shrugged. "My gut tells me yes. Could I prove it? No way."

Michael shoved his hands through his hair and exchanged a look with the two policemen. "So where the hell does that leave us?"

Ken leaned forward. "I do have one idea. I've got some time coming."

"Forget it," Michael said.

Ken continued as if he hadn't spoken, his expression determined. "I could take leave for the next day or two and do a little diving out where the boat blew up. Maybe I'll find something the others missed."

Michael shook his head. "No way." At a scowl from Molly, he modified his harsh response. "Thanks, but you know those guys combed the bottom for whatever was big enough to be recognizable. I don't want you wasting your leave time like that. You've got a wife and kid who'd never forgive me if your vacation time comes up short."

Ken shrugged. "Hell, you know Teri. She loves to dive even more than I do. She'll be thrilled to have an unexpected excuse to take our boat out in the middle of the week."

"Don't you suppose she'd rather be checking out a coral reef?" Michael asked.

Ken grinned. "I'll explain that this is more challenging."

"Are you sure you want to spend your time off this way?" Michael asked again, his voice filled with doubt. For the first time, though, it also held a wavering hint of hope.

"A boat, a sunny day, my wife in a bikini, a couple of beers," Ken replied. "Does life get any better than that?"

"No, I suppose not," Michael agreed. He held out his hand and clasped Ken's. "Thanks. I really appreciate it."

"No problem. I'll give you a call as soon as I work out the details."

"So what can I do?" Felipe asked. "I'd take leave time, too, but you know I use it as fast as I accumulate it."

Ken rolled his eyes. "He means that every time he gets a hot date, he can't drag himself out of bed to leave her. The time sheets tell the story of his love life."

Felipe muttered something in Spanish that definitely didn't sound complimentary, but both Ken and Michael were laughing. Felipe glanced at Molly. "Excuse them. Neither of them understand how demanding it is to be both single and sexy," he said, his eyes glinting with pure mischief.

"I'm single," Michael reminded him.

Felipe shrugged. "But sexy? That is a matter of opinion."

Michael turned toward Molly. She held up her hands. "No comment."

"Et tu, Brute?" he said. "You will pay for that, *amiga.*"

"I didn't realize my role here was to stroke your ego," Molly retorted.

"Perhaps we should discuss precisely what your role here is," Michael replied, his eyes flashing dangerously.

"Uh-oh," Ken said, standing up. "Come on, Felipe. Let some other cop get called to deal with this domestic disturbance. I want no part of it."

"No disturbance," Michael said mildly.

"And it's not domestic," Molly chimed in, her cheeks flaming.

The two cops exchanged glances. Felipe held a hand over his stomach. "My very reliable gut thinks we've got two people here who are protesting too much."

Molly suddenly wondered if it might not be a very good idea to ask if she could hitch a ride home. The gleam in Michael's eyes stopped her before the words could form.

When both men had beat a hasty exit, Michael strolled back into the living room. He reached out and clasped Molly's hand, hauling her to her feet. He didn't let go until she was mere inches away, so close, in fact, that she could feel the heat radiating from his body. His gaze clashed with hers.

"So, *amiga,* you think I am not sexy?"

"I didn't say that."

"Oh?"

"Not exactly."

"Then you think I am sexy?"

"I think you are deliberately trying to intimidate a witness."

"You're no witness. You're the perpetrator here."

"Oh, yeah? What's the crime?"

"Lying under oath."

Molly glanced around. "No judge. No jury. No Bible. I'd say you have no case, mister."

He gave her a wry look and laced his fingers through the hair at the nape of her neck. Very slowly he drew her toward him. Only when Molly thought she would never catch her breath again did he slant his mouth over hers.

She had to admit, as she tried to prevent herself from swaying straight into his arms, that it was a very expert kiss. One of the best, in fact. She was also determined that Michael would never, not in a million years, badger that admission out of her. It was, of course, okay with her if he wanted to kiss her from now until doomsday in an attempt to torture the words from her.

The shrill sound of the phone finally forced them apart. From her perspective, it was probably a very timely interruption.

"Yes, what?" Michael demanded gruffly, one arm still looped around her waist as he talked to the caller.

Molly couldn't seem to tear her gaze away. That was probably why she was so quick to note the sudden alertness in his eyes and the tightening of his jaw.

"I'm on my way," he said, already reaching for his gun and jacket as he hung up.

Molly grabbed her purse and raced out the door after him. Apparently he'd expected her to follow automatically, because he never said a single thing to encourage or protest it. Not until they were in his car and pulling out of the driveway into the traffic on Kendall did she ask where they were going.

"To the paper."

"Why?"

"That was your pal Ted Ryan. He says there are about fifty protesters in front of the building, trying to prevent the delivery trucks from going out.''

"Why did he call you?''

"Because someone down there said these guys are all followers of Paredes.''

CHAPTER
TEN

Even at eleven at night there was still plenty of traffic to contend with between Kendall and downtown. Though Michael drove like a cop after a speeding suspect, it took them close to thirty minutes before they squealed around a corner and screeched to a stop a half block away from the paper.

Just as Ted Ryan had told Michael, protesters blocked the streets leading into and away from the loading dock. The paper's trucks, parked in solid rows along the street and in an adjacent lot, were effectively prevented from leaving the area. The signs carried by the relatively small group of protesters were in Spanish and in English. Those Molly could read protested the unfairness of the paper's coverage. It was a fairly general and oft-repeated charge.

As they left the car, Michael glanced at her. "Why don't you see if you can hook up with Ryan and see what this is all about? I'm going to try to blend in and see what I can learn from the protesters."

Molly didn't think there was much chance that Michael, still wearing his usual designer suit and expensive shirt, could actually blend in with what at first glance looked to be a ragtag band of aging male picketers, many of whom were wearing military fatigues and waving Cuban flags. Still, with his dark complexion, brown eyes, and dark hair, there was no mistaking that Hispanic blood ran in his veins. Maybe that would be enough to loosen tongues.

She wandered closer, finally selecting a car right at the edge of the protest and leaning against the front bumper. From that vantage point, she realized that there was more diversity among those picketing than she had originally thought. She caught sight of at least three younger men, clad in dress pants, shirts, and ties, and several women who also looked like young professionals. The broader cross-section of the exile community surprised her. Maybe Ted Ryan would be able to explain it.

She figured it would be only a matter of minutes before he spotted her. The reporter tended to zero in on her like a homing pigeon. Usually, though, he was after information. Tonight Molly intended to turn the tables. She found she was actually looking forward to transforming a member of the aggressive media into a source. In her job at the film office she so rarely had a chance to make that happen. Vince insisted on a lot of bowing and scraping.

As she'd anticipated, she saw Ted Ryan circle the perimeter of the protesters, pause for a minute under a streetlamp to jot down some notes, then gaze up and down the street. The instant he spotted her, he headed in her direction. His boyish grin widened as he reached her. He looked more like an amiable Clark Kent than a determined Mike Wallace, but Molly knew firsthand that in his case looks were deceiving. Ted had the tenacity of a pit bull.

"I saw O'Hara a minute ago," he said. "I figured you wouldn't be far away." He regarded her intently. "Just how close are you two these days?" he asked with an unusual hint of uncertainty in his voice.

"I like to think of it as a partnership," Molly said dryly. "My guess is Michael would call it something else."

The reporter seemed even more disconcerted by the comment. "A partnership as in wedding bells?"

"No, as in investigative colleagues."

There was no mistaking the look of relief in Ted's eyes, which confirmed what Michael had been telling Molly for some time: Ted Ryan might have the teeniest little crush on her. Until this instant, Molly had dismissed it as hogwash. Apparently, though, this was the one thing territorial males were capable of sensing instinctively about other men. Since she wasn't prepared to deal with whatever personal interest Ted might have in her, she changed the subject quickly.

"Thanks for calling Michael with the tip about the demonstration. Why did you?"

The reporter accepted the shift in topic almost gratefully. "Don't credit me with being too magnanimous. He's always in the middle of the hottest cases in town. I figured one of these days he'll return the favor and give me a break on a story. Besides, something tells me this protest and what happened to his uncle can't be coincidence."

"Meaning?"

"His uncle worked for circulation, delivering the papers. The last time anyone saw him, as far as we know, was when he met his route supervisor to get the Sunday edition. Now, just two nights later, we've got the makings of a big-time brouhaha on our front lawn involving what appears to be the same group of exiles in which García was involved."

Molly pointed to the picket signs. "What exactly do they think is unfair about the paper's coverage?"

Ted shook his head. "Hell, sometimes it seems to me they object to anything that isn't violently anti-Castro. Who knows what it's about this time.''

Molly regarded him doubtfully. She didn't like the way he was evading her gaze. "Come on, Ted. You're a reporter. Even if you didn't work for this particular paper, you'd make it your business to know every last detail of any controversy in which the media was targeted. So what's with the vague generalities?''

He shook his head. "I'm telling you there's nothing specific I can link this to. I even read the damned Spanish-language edition, which took me hours, I might add, to see if I could figure out why they're bent out of shape. We're not supporting some bill on Capitol Hill that's soft on Castro. We haven't attacked any of their sacred cows. The most controversial story I saw, from their perspective, was another one of those statistical things showing how many Cuban rafters have been welcomed by Immigration and how many boatloads of Haitian refugees have been turned back at sea. They don't like being reminded that the difference in policies seems blatantly discriminatory.''

Molly didn't buy that as the cause of tonight's incident. She wished she'd read that morning's edition, but in all the confusion she hadn't had time. She tried to recall anything else she had read in the paper in recent days that could have set things off. "Wasn't there a story in the business pages about a couple of companies that have sent people into Cuba to size up economic opportunities?"

"Yes, but so what? The way economic sanctions are, they can't go in and invest until Castro falls, right?"

Molly sighed. "True. Maybe the protesters are objecting to the fact that these guys spent dollars in Cuba while they were over there scouting things out. You know how violent they get about foreign tourists in Cuba. They feel the money the tourists spend helps to shore up Castro's regime."

Ted shook his head. "Then why not protest the companies, rather than the paper that wrote the story?"

Molly didn't have an argument to counter that. She tried out another thought. "Has the paper backed any cultural events lately?"

"Like what?"

"You know how they're always giving money to support the ballet, the opera, and all these ethnic festivals. I was just wondering if they'd made a donation to something like that and the group in turn had invited a performer who'd recently performed in Cuba."

"I doubt it. I think the paper's gotten real sensitive to that sort of thing. The powers that be may not understand why people get so outraged that a singer or dancer has performed in Havana, but they steer clear of them just the same."

They fell silent then, watching the activity of

the demonstrators, until Ted spotted someone in the crowd and called out to him. The man, wearing khaki slacks, a blue oxford-cloth shirt, and loafers, looked to be no more than forty, though his dark blond hair was already thinning on top. He jogged over to join them.

"Hey, Ted, what's up?"

Ted regarded the older reporter with something akin to hero worship. "Molly, this is Walt Hazelton. He's working the story. He's been with the paper fifteen years. For the last ten he's been on the foreign desk covering Caribbean affairs, including Cuba, when they'll grant him a visa to go in. Walt, this is Molly DeWitt. She and O'Hara are friends."

Walt nodded. "I thought I saw him nosing around in the crowd." He looked at Molly. "Any word on his uncle?"

Molly shook her head. "How good are your sources inside Cuba?" she asked. She knew from his highly respected reputation for hard-hitting, award-winning coverage that Walt Hazelton wasn't the sort of journalist who'd rely on rumors, but rather would report only carefully gleaned facts. She suspected he'd made good use of those rarely granted trips to the island to cultivate reliable contacts.

Hazelton's eyes widened as he immediately grasped her meaning. "You think García tried to go in, maybe as part of some commando raid?"

"It's one theory. I just wondered if you knew

anyone who might know what's going on on the island?"

The reporter looked thoughtful. "No one else has been reported missing here in town."

"Maybe because no one else has a nephew like Michael, who jumped on his uncle's disappearance immediately," she countered, beginning to warm to the theory. "Maybe that boat was meant to blow up at sea, so there'd be no trace after they'd launched their rafts toward shore. And wouldn't any family members here be warned to remain silent?"

"Did you get the feeling O'Hara's aunt was holding back?" Ted asked.

Molly honestly had no answer to that. She didn't know Tía Pilar well enough to judge when she might be withholding information. Their conversations were conducted in such a halting mix of English and Spanish that they were seldom illuminating anyway. She finally shook her head. "I have no idea."

"It could take a while to get through, but I'll do some checking," Hazelton promised. He reached in his pocket and pulled out a card. "Give me a call tomorrow afternoon."

When he'd walked away, Molly stared after him. "Bright guy. I've read about him. He's picked up several awards for his reporting, hasn't he?"

"A Pulitzer and a bunch of others," Ted agreed. "He deserves every one of them. He's got an advanced degree in international studies. Had a fellowship to study Cuba." He gestured toward the crowd, who were now chanting and waving their signs more aggressively. "Hazelton probably knows more about the island today than half of these protesters ever knew about the way it was thirty, thirty-five years ago when they were last there. They hate his guts, though."

"Why?"

"Do you even have to ask? He's not one of them. Worse than not being Cuban, he dares to tell it like it is. He's not keeping the dream alive."

As if to confirm what Ted was saying, apparently someone recognized Hazelton just then. Before Molly could blink, they had surrounded him, making demands, shouting curses. One angry man waved his picket sign threateningly. Hazelton shoved his way through the crowd and made his way to the building entrance. A police escort saw that he made it.

"I can hardly wait to see the final edition," Ted said dryly.

"Do you think this demonstration will be broken up in time for anyone to see it?" Molly asked.

"Oh, the paper will be printed and it will go out," Ted said, regarding the scene with blatant disgust. "In another hour or two the publisher will lose patience, the police will cordon off the road, and the trucks will roll. The paper may be late, but believe me, these bullies won't be allowed to stop it. It amazes me how people can flee a country with no freedom of the press, then try to stifle it in the country that takes them in."

"What about freedom of speech and freedom to assemble?" Molly countered quietly.

Ted looked at her. "Hey, I have no problem with them protesting. They've got a right to voice their opinions like anyone else. What they don't have is the right to violently prevent me from voicing mine or the paper from voicing its views editorially."

Molly figured it wasn't a debate that was going to be won or lost that night, any more than it was won or lost when opposition sides of the abortion debate clashed on the lawns of abortion clinics. She suspected emotions ran equally high in both controversies.

"You told Michael these protesters were followers of Paredes," she said finally.

"Some of them. I recognize them from other rallies. The others could be part of his organization or representatives of some other groups."

"Is Paredes here?"

"Are you kidding? He's out in Westchester watching it all on TV, happy as a clam at the disruption of the paper's delivery schedule. No doubt, if questioned, he will decry the harassment of Hazelton."

"Just as he decried the bombing of Miguel's boat."

131

"Of course. But just because there's no dirt under a guy's fingernails doesn't mean he knows nothing about the seeds being sown in this particular garden of protest."

Molly grinned. "Interesting line. Can I expect to read it in tomorrow's paper?"

Ted grinned back at her. "Not in my story. I'm on page one of the Metro section with a fascinating report on two cops whose police car was stolen while they sipped *café Cubano* on *Calle Ocho*. It seems the driver left the keys in the ignition, thinking his partner was going to stay put. Said partner decided he wanted to join his pal at the take-out window. An alert bystander in need of wheels made off with it before either of them could draw their weapons. Needless to say the two were not available for interviews. I suspect they've been checked into the county hospital, where they're dying of embarrassment."

Molly heard only about half of the story Ted was telling. She'd suddenly noticed the delivery truck drivers who were all gathered around their vehicles in a lot across the street awaiting an end to the protest.

"Ted, thanks again for the tip tonight," she said distractedly, her attention already focused on the drivers.

"Hey, where are you going?"

"To find Miguel's route supervisor."

"I'll come with you," he said at once, hurrying after her.

132

She glanced back at him. "Okay, but I ask the questions."

He regarded her with clearly feigned indignation. "Hey, who's the reporter here?"

"You're off duty, remember?"

"Dammit, Molly, O'Hara will kill me if you get into a bind asking questions of the wrong person."

"I am not your responsibility," she reminded him. "I'm not Michael's either, for that matter. Last I heard, I had God-given free will."

"Jesus, we've gone from Constitutional rights to the big time," Ted said. "How are you going to find this guy? You don't even know his name, do you?"

"No, but I know where Miguel's route was. He delivered to the houses in the Shenandoah section. That's why he kept his boat on Key Biscayne. He could drive straight over the causeway when he finished his deliveries and be on the water by dawn."

Fortunately, all of the route bosses were clustered in one place. It took only one casually asked inquiry to find the man who supervised the Shenandoah area deliveries. He was a cigar-chomping, overweight hulk of a man who identified himself as Jack Miller. He looked at Ted, his gaze narrowed.

"You're that guy we ran the campaign on a few months back, aren't you? Had your picture on the trucks. Ryan, right?"

Ted nodded, his expression pleased. The recognition apparently served to overcome his reservations about Molly's interviewing the guy. He turned downright expansive, in fact, introducing her as if she were his personal protégée.

Miller removed his cigar from his mouth long enough to mutter a greeting. "You looking for me?"

She nodded. "I'm wondering about Miguel García. Are you his supervisor?"

His gaze narrowed suspiciously. "Now why would you want to know something like that? You a TV reporter? I don't see no camera."

"I'm not a reporter. I'm a close friend of his family's, and it occurred to me that you might have been one of the last people to see him before he disappeared."

Some of his suspicion melted away. "Could be," he conceded.

She decided she'd better seize that scant opening and run with it. "He worked Sunday morning?"

"Like clockwork. He's been one of my best employees."

"Always on time?"

"The man has the constitution of a horse. He's never missed a day I can think of, not without sending somebody to cover his route anyway."

"What did you think when he didn't show up last night?"

He shrugged. "I didn't think nothing. He wasn't supposed to work."

Molly regarded him with surprise. "He wasn't?"

"No, ma'am. Took vacation. Asked for it a month ago at least."

"How long was he supposed to be off?"

"Two weeks is what he told me. No matter what's gone on, I fully expect him to show up. García's the kind of man I'd rely on if my life depended on it."

"So there was nothing on Sunday you thought was suspicious, nothing in his demeanor that was out of character?"

Miller hesitated over the question, as if he were chewing it over in his head. "Now that I think back on it, there was one thing. Pardon me for saying it, but anyone else I'd have said they were getting lucky." He looked at Molly. "You know what I'm talking about?" At her nod, he continued, "I've seen that look with guys who have something going on on the side. Not García, though. He loved that wife of his. Talked about her all the time."

"What was different about him on Sunday?"

"He looked real happy. Never saw him look that way before, you know what I mean?"

"As if he was looking forward to something," Molly suggested.

Miller bobbed his head. "Exactly. Like he couldn't wait for something special that was going to happen. Like a kid on Christmas morning, you know?''

"Or maybe a man who was going home to Cuba," she said softly.

CHAPTER
ELEVEN

As Ted Ryan had predicted, the Miami police moved the demonstration into a contained area shortly after one A.M. and the newspaper's delivery trucks began to roll. Before long, with their audience dwindling and their effectiveness stymied, the protesters began to pack up and leave themselves. Michael's expression was grim when he joined Molly and the reporter.

"Did you find out anything?" Molly asked him.

"You mean besides the fact that this paper is run by racist Commies?"

"My boss, the devoted Republican, will be thrilled to know that," Ted said dryly. "Obviously, his journalistic evenhandedness is paying off. He's clearly not inflicting his conservative views on the reading public."

Michael shot a look at the reporter that Molly found troubling. "You did find out what this was all about, didn't you? I mean beyond the usual rhetoric."

"You mean Ryan here hasn't told you?"

"Told me what?"

"It was his story today that set them off. Apparently they felt his portrayal of Miguel made him look like part of some lunatic-fringe organization."

Ted paled at that. "I didn't write anything that wasn't absolutely true," he argued.

Molly began to understand why he'd been so evasive earlier. She also recognized just from the comments he'd made to her that he held certain Anglo prejudices that might very well have come through in his reporting. Alone the story might have been viewed as an example of biased reporting. Added to dozens of other articles, it had triggered a protest. She couldn't blame Ted for wanting to downplay his role in the night's events.

"Look, let's just forget about what started the protest," she suggested. "We need to focus on Miguel. Were you able to learn anything about his disappearance from any of Paredes's backers?"

"No. Trying to talk to these guys was an absolute waste of time," Michael said. "I know damn well that they know something about what hap-

138

pened to Tío Miguel, but they'll deny it with their dying breaths."

"Maybe this was the wrong place to confront them," Molly suggested. "Here they're unified. Naturally no one would break ranks and spill the beans. Did you get names, addresses, phone numbers?"

"From the ones who would tell me," he said, his voice filled with frustration. "Since I wasn't here on official business, I couldn't force them even to give me that much."

"So you'll start tomorrow with the ones who did identify themselves," she said. "Where are your notes?"

"What for?"

"So I can give the names to Ted," she explained patiently. "He can check them out in the newspaper's files and with the foreign desk to see if any of them are prime movers and shakers among the exile groups."

"I could do the same thing at the police station," he countered with a stubborn set to his jaw.

Molly wasn't sure if he was behaving like a jerk because she was trying to involve Ted Ryan —his perceived competition for her affections— in the investigation or if he was just plain exhausted. She decided to assume it was the latter. On two hours' sleep, it was a logical enough assumption. And that conclusion was the only thing enabling her to continue her fragile grip on her patience.

"And then we'll have two angles on the situation, won't we?" she replied quietly.

He scowled at her. "I suppose." He handed over his notes and allowed Ted to copy the names.

"I'll get right on it," Ted said. "Where should I call you?"

"My place," Molly and Michael said simultaneously. They were not referring to the same place.

This time she glared at him. "Mine is closer. You're beat and so am I."

"Okay, fine. Whatever," Michael said. He looked at Ted and added grudgingly, "Thanks for calling earlier."

"No problem. I'll speak to you in the morning. Maybe Walt will have some news by then too."

"Night, Ted," Molly said.

"Who's Walt?" Michael asked as they walked back to his car.

"Hazelton. He's their chief foreign correspondent for the Caribbean. He's making some calls into Cuba to see if there's any word there about armed guerrillas sneaking onto the island."

"Molly, as much as I'd like to believe otherwise, I don't think Miguel went back to Cuba."

140

"Twenty-four hours ago that was all you were willing to consider," she reminded him.

"That was before the boat blew to smithereens."

"Then you should have been around when I talked with Tío Miguel's supervisor. He says when he saw him on Sunday morning, he looked happier than he'd ever seen him, like a man who might be going home again."

Michael regarded her in disbelief. "You're basing this cock-and-bull theory on the fact that my uncle was in a good mood, for God's sake? The man was always in a good mood."

"This was different," Molly insisted, refusing to be put off by his skepticism. "Jack Miller could see it and, believe me, he doesn't strike me as a man prone to intuitive guesswork. There had to be some real change in your uncle's demeanor for him to notice it. Haven't you ever noticed that for all of his apparent good humor, Tío Miguel's eyes always look kind of sad and faraway?"

"I suppose," Michael conceded wearily.

"I think we need to talk to your aunt again tomorrow."

"I was planning on it, but you obviously have something specific in mind. What?"

"I think we need to see if she suspects that your uncle has gone back to Cuba, but is afraid to admit it because it might jeopardize some grand scheme these guys have."

"Don't you think she would have told me that?"

"Not if she was afraid that telling would put him in greater danger or might even put you in danger. Don't you remember, when you called her on Sunday afternoon, you said yourself she sounded as if she was worried about something. You detected it in her voice. That's why you were so hell-bent on looking for him right away. Isn't it possible she knew what he was up to?"

Michael looked thoughtful. "You could be right. If that's the case, though, we won't pry it out of her. We'll have to talk to Tía Elena."

Now Molly was having trouble following his logic. "Why her?"

"Because Miguel might have confided in Tío Pedro. Pedro won't break a confidence to talk to me, but he keeps nothing from his wife. Pilar would know that, as well, and she might even have confided in her sister. That's two people talking to Elena."

"And you have always been able to wheedle anything you wanted from her, right?"

He grinned. "I am her favorite nephew, after all."

Molly shook her head. "I can't imagine why."

He reached over, clasped her hand and lifted it to his lips. "Sure you can, *amiga*. No one is more aware of my charms than you."

With a sudden leap of her pulse, Molly decided tonight might be a good night to find out exactly how *charming* Michael O'Hara could be . . . if either of them could stay awake long enough.

Apparently Michael intended to give it a try, because he took her hand when they left the car and didn't release it until they were in her bedroom.

"So, *amiga*, how do you feel about finishing what you began in my bedroom earlier today?" he said.

Molly met his serious gaze. "I thought you'd never ask."

His hands framed her face. "We have waited a long time for this, *querida*. We could probably have found a better time, a better night."

She felt herself smiling. "Don't start making excuses for yourself, O'Hara."

"I will need no excuses," he assured her with a touch of macho arrogance that made Molly's heart hammer at its promise.

"And here I was so sure you were out of practice."

"There are some things a man never forgets," he said quietly just as his lips met hers.

With his mouth teaching her amazing nuances of the art of the kiss and his hands deftly exploring other parts of her anatomy, Molly was in no position to argue. In fact, she wondered as they scrambled out of their clothes and into the bed, if Michael would be willing to continue

burning the basics into her memory from now
till doomsday.

• • •

It didn't come as a great shock to Molly that even
on one of his worst nights, when he was fighting
bone-deep exhaustion, Michael was hotter and
more thoughtful in bed than the wildest fantasy
she had ever had. The man had amazing
reserves of stamina and the touch of a sinner.

Unfortunately it also came as no surprise
that he was all business in the morning.

"Let's go, *amiga,*" he said after what had to
have been no more than fifteen minutes of unin-
terrupted sleep.

Molly mumbled something derogatory and
tried to hide under the covers. He smacked her
on the bottom and repeated his demand.

"Coffee's on and the train leaves in twenty
minutes," he announced.

Molly blinked, inched the covers down to
her chin and peered up at him. "What train?"

"It's a figure of speech. Do you want to sleep
all day or do you want to help me find my uncle?"

It was a toss-up, she decided. But given the
way she'd groused until he included her as a
partner in the investigation, she couldn't bail
out now just so she could indulge in some sleepy,
steamy reminiscences about the night just past.

Twenty minutes later on the dot, Michael was

waiting for her at the front door, a cup of coffee in hand.

"Toast?" she suggested hopefully.

"No time. We'll stop later. I want to catch Luis Díaz-Nuñez before he leaves the radio station."

Molly had forgotten all about the controversial commentator. She had plenty of time to recall his vitriolic personality over the next half hour since Michael kept the car radio tuned to his station as they drove across the causeway and along Coral Way until they reached the broadcast studio. She didn't understand most of Díaz-Nuñez's words, but there was no mistaking the tenor. The morning paper was mentioned often enough for her to guess he had taken up the cause of the previous night's demonstrators.

At the station Molly waited for Michael to try to relegate her to another wait in the car. To her astonishment, he didn't say a word. He just walked around and opened her door.

"You want me to go in?" she asked with undisguised astonishment.

"Something tells me your presence will rattle Díaz-Nuñez."

"Why?"

He grinned. "You are not aware of his reputation?"

"As a commentator, yes," she said.

"He also regards himself as quite a ladies' man. I'm hoping he'll be so engrossed in the

145

amusement of trying to seduce you under my very eyes that he'll be less cautious in the answers he gives me."

"And here I thought you wanted to take advantage of my great interrogation skills."

"Oh, feel free to chime in anytime. Just don't expect him to take you seriously. He is not exactly a modern, liberated male when it comes to his views of women."

Molly detected an odd note in his voice. "Just how well do you know this guy?"

"Well enough," Michael replied curtly.

"Obviously you don't have much respect for him. Why would you know him so well?"

"He was involved with my cousin Ileana for a while. I figure another three years of recovery and she'll have her self-esteem back."

"And you want to throw me to this wolf?"

He squeezed her hand reassuringly. "Never, *amiga*. I just wish to dangle the bait, so to speak."

She frowned at him. "What a pleasant prospect."

• • •

In his pin-striped suit and designer loafers, Luis Díaz-Nuñez was younger than Molly had anticipated, maybe in his early forties, and definitely more polished. With his prematurely gray hair, olive complexion, soulful brown eyes, and a smile that transformed his face, he was also better looking. Her heart did a dutiful little pit-a-patter, just as he'd no doubt intended. She could see that flirting was as much second nature to him as cross-examining people was to Michael.

He ushered Michael and Molly into a cramped office cluttered with Spanish-language newspapers and magazines. On the wall were framed photographs of the newscaster with President Reagan, President Bush, and the head of the powerful Cuban-American National Foundation. Clearly this was a man with ties to Washington. No doubt his radio show had given these same political creatures access to a huge Cuban audience that they needed to win support in South Florida.

"It is a terrible thing about your uncle's boat," he said to Michael when they were seated. All the while his gaze was on Molly. On her legs, to be precise. He finally blinked and looked back at Michael. "Do you know who is behind it?"

Michael shook his head. "I thought perhaps you might have some ideas."

Molly leaned forward, a movement that gave her the opportunity to tug her skirt over her knees without being too obvious about it. "Yes, Michael's been telling me how influential your radio show is and what terrific sources you have in the exile community. Surely you have heard things." She made it a statement, rather than a question.

"I have many friends, yes," he agreed, picking up a thin cigar from his desk and running his long fingers over it in a gesture that was obscenely sensual. His eyes met hers and he shrugged. "But about this I have heard nothing."

"What is your good friend Paredes up to these days?" Michael inquired bluntly. Too bluntly, judging from the closed expression that suddenly came over Díaz-Nuñez's face.

Molly jumped in again. "He's a fascinating man, isn't he? I've met him only once, but I was struck with the aura of self-confidence about him. It is difficult these days to find men who are so committed to any cause."

The newscaster's gaze locked with hers. "You admire commitment?"

"Of course. It is the true measure of a man, don't you think?"

"Absolutely. And you are correct about Paredes. He has a vision and he will not rest until it becomes a reality."

"The fall of Castro," Molly said.

"That, yes, but more importantly, the restoration of our homeland to its prior glory. He will be at the forefront of such a recovery."

"And for this he has a plan, no doubt?" she continued, grateful that Michael seemed willing to let her try to seduce answers from Díaz-Nuñez.

"But of course," he said.

"Has he begun to implement this plan?"

The newscaster suddenly snapped the cigar in two and tossed the shredded pieces onto his desk. His gaze was no longer nearly as friendly.

"Mrs. DeWitt, whatever plans Paredes has he will reveal when the time is right," he said coldly. "We are waging a war here, not orchestrating some children's playground skirmish."

Molly refused to let his sharp retort or the sudden coldness in his eyes daunt her. "I understand that some of his men are already in place inside Cuba."

Díaz-Nuñez glanced at Michael. "Do you always allow your woman to speak for you?" he inquired with an air of macho derision.

Molly flinched at the deliberate rebuff. Apparently he'd merely been humoring her and had tired of it. She had a few things she wouldn't mind saying to him about his attitude, but fortunately Michael jumped into the fray before she could get started.

"I do when she's asking all the right questions," he said quietly. "You must find such questions troubling or you wouldn't be shifting the subject so readily."

Díaz-Nuñez's jaw tensed at the insult. "Perhaps, then, I should give you a word of advice," he said, regarding Michael intently. "These questions are dangerous ones, my friend. This is a delicate time when the future of our homeland may very well hang in the balance." His gaze shifted to Molly. "Anyone who threatens this will be disposed of like that," he added with a decisive snap of his fingers.

A chill shot down Molly's back. Michael, however, leaned forward and met Díaz-Nuñez's gaze evenly. "If I learn that anyone involved with this so-called delicate operation has harmed one hair on my uncle's head, or if anyone dares to threaten anyone close to me again, then hell will be a pleasant alternative to the fate I will inflict."

Díaz-Nuñez visibly withered under the lethal intensity of Michael's warning.

Michael stood up, his gaze leveled on the man who had remained seated. "I assume we understand each other, my *friend*," he said in a way that could not be interpreted as friendly.

"Most definitely," the newscaster said without meeting his gaze.

Molly figured the proof of that could be found in the way he continued to keep his eyes averted as they left his office. The kind of man to whom studying a woman's tush was second nature, Díaz-Nuñez suddenly seemed totally absorbed in cleaning up the crushed cigar tobacco that littered his desk.

CHAPTER
TWELVE

When Michael cut across town on Twenty-seventh Avenue toward Little Havana, Molly gathered they were going to see his family. She decided she needed sustenance before that happened. Her brain cells functioned more efficiently with a little protein and caffeine to charge them.

"You promised me breakfast," she reminded him.

"McDonald's?"

"Not on your life."

"Cuban coffee and a cheese-and-guava pastry?"

"Better."

"Good. Those you can get at Tía Pilar's."

"Too cheap to buy me breakfast," she noted. "I'll remember that."

"Not cheap, *amiga*. Just in a hurry. Time is passing too quickly, and with each hour that passes, I grow more concerned for Miguel. The sooner I speak with Elena, the sooner perhaps I will have new leads."

Molly's teasing ended at once. "Of course. I'm sorry. How do you plan on getting your aunt to talk if everyone's all together at Tía Pilar's? She'll never admit to anything with her husband and sister looking on."

"I'll manage. It's possible Pedro may not even be there. He's probably opening the restaurant again today." He glanced at her worriedly. "You haven't said a word about our meeting with Díaz-Nuñez. Usually you can't wait to dissect every word, every nuance, of a conversation."

"What do you expect me to say? That the guy gave me the creeps? Are you waiting for me to demand a device so I can check my car before I turn on the ignition?"

"It wouldn't be a bad idea," he said.

His tone was far more serious than Molly would have preferred. "Surely you don't take his threat seriously?" she asked, hoping for a denial.

"Yes, I do."

The blunt, matter-of-fact reply chilled her. "But I thought it was a standoff. You warned him what would happen if he or anyone else did anything."

"You don't understand, *amiga*. To a man like Díaz-Nuñez or to Paredes, the cause is more important than any individual's life, even their own."

"But he's a newscaster, for God's sake. A journalist."

Michael shrugged. "That label does not mean the same thing to him that it does to you. He is as much an advocate of revolution as Paredes. He learned his attitudes at his father's knee. When Raúl Díaz was killed during the Bay of Pigs, Luis made the cause his own. He and his friends would not hesitate to silence anyone perceived as a threat to their goals, and they would be prepared to suffer the consequences."

"But that's . . ." Molly fumbled for a suitable word. "Barbaric."

"In their view, it is warfare."

"I thought such extremist views had died out in the seventies and eighties, even among those most violently opposed to Castro."

"Such passion seldom dissipates. If anything, it only grows stronger the longer the ultimate goal remains elusive. How many times have they had their hopes raised, only to see Castro's strength overcome the odds? Too many by their count. If they again decide terrorist tactics are necessary . . ." He shrugged. "And make no mistake, the average Cuban may disapprove of the violence but will understand its cause."

"You don't."

"Perhaps it is my Irish blood," he said with a shrug. "Or perhaps I was too young when I left.

Maybe it is just that as a policeman, I deplore violence of any kind and can make no excuses for it."

Molly thought of Brian, who was currently safe with her ex-husband. Obviously this was one time when it would be not only foolish but irresponsible to bring him home as long as the threat of danger continued. Michael was not an alarmist. If he believed so strongly that she was in danger, then she had to take it seriously, even if the threat was beyond her comprehension.

"I'll have to leave Brian with Hal for a while longer, won't I?"

He glanced over at her. "It would probably be best. And you will stay with me. No arguments, okay?"

Molly thought of the hard, cold expression in Díaz-Nuñez's eyes when he had snapped that cigar in two and shivered. "No arguments."

● ● ●

From what Molly could observe, Tía Elena was not nearly as forthcoming as Michael had anticipated her being. If anything, she was downright coy, denying that anyone had mentioned a word to her about what she referred to indifferently as "political matters."

Michael regarded her with evident frustration. "You are not helping Miguel by staying silent."

154

"If I knew something of consequence, do you not think I would tell you?" she retorted.

"Pedro has said nothing to you?"

"How many times must I tell you this?"

"Your own sister has not confided in you?"

"My sister is inconsolable with grief. She weeps for her husband. She does not waste time on foolish speculation."

Molly watched Tía Elena's round face as she spoke and listened to the rhythm of her words. There was an almost indiscernible hesitation that only someone listening so intently would have heard. Michael clearly was less attuned to the subtle change.

Molly placed her hand over the older woman's. She had grown genuinely fond of Michael's aunt, and she thought the feeling was reciprocated. Perhaps it was time for less bullying tactics and more woman-to-woman compassion. "But Pilar has speculated, hasn't she?" she said softly.

Michael's aunt met her gaze and her lips trembled slightly. She shot a worried glance at her nephew. "They were the words of a woman who is crazy with worry," she finally admitted with obvious reluctance.

Molly persisted. "Perhaps so, but isn't it possible that she knows something in her heart, even if Tío Miguel never confirmed it."

"What did she tell you?" Michael asked, and this time his own tone was more gentle. The man

155

was nothing if not adaptable. "*Por favor*, Elena? Please."

Elena sighed heavily. "She heard things, in the night when Miguel thought she was asleep. There were men here, arguing, planning, whatever. She could not be sure. She had heard such talk before. Pipe dreams, that is all they were. Surely, no one would attempt such foolishness," Elena said with more hope than conviction.

"An attack?" Michael said. "They were planning to invade Cuba?"

Maria sighed again and gazed toward the heavens, as if for guidance. At last she nodded. "That is what she thought."

"Did she see these men? Was Paredes one of them?"

"She did not say, not to me anyway."

Michael's jaw firmed. "She will tell me."

Elena touched his arm. "She will not, not if she believes it could mean endangering Miguel."

"He is already in danger," Michael snapped. He shoved his hand through his hair. "Dammit, I don't understand this. I don't understand him."

It was the cry of a man one generation removed from the heartache of exile.

● ● ●

Tía Pilar regarded her nephew with a stoic expression. Not all of Michael's gentle cajoling or impatient badgering had been able to shake a single word from her. Not by so much as the flicker of an eyelash did she react when he said he knew that she had overheard something the night before Miguel's disappearance.

"Why won't you tell me?" he said yet again.

"No sé," she insisted as she had since the questions had begun. She knew nothing.

Molly touched Michael's arm and shot him an imploring look. With a curt nod he allowed her to take over.

"Tía Pilar, do you have photographs from Cuba?"

The old woman listened carefully, her ability to translate the English words as halting now as it probably had been when she'd arrived more than thirty years before. Molly touched a framed picture of Miguel sitting on the table by her chair. "More pictures from Cuba?"

She nodded emphatically and her expression softened. *"Sí, sí."*

She stood up and went to a breakfront in the tiny dining room. When she returned, she carried an album. Molly moved to her side. Pilar motioned for Michael to join them. He looked as if he wanted to protest that they were wasting precious time, but he finally relented and hunkered down beside the chair.

Then with great ceremony Pilar opened the book to the first page. Molly felt as if she'd been transported back in time by the black-and-white snapshots and more formal portraits pasted so lovingly into the album, each with a description under it in precise handwriting.

"My parents," Pilar said haltingly, pointing to the lovely dark-haired girl, who wore a cameo at the throat of her lace-trimmed, high-necked blouse, and the solemn man standing formally behind her. "At their wedding."

Pilar glanced at Michael for a reaction. Molly caught the suspicious sheen of tears in his eyes. "You remember them, don't you?" she asked.

He nodded. "I never saw them again after I was sent to this country. My grandfather died right after that. And then, two years later, my grandmother," he said in a voice thick with emotion. "My grandmother was always laughing. That's what I remember when I think of Cuba, not the beauty of the countryside or the way of life, but the sound of her laughter."

Pilar carefully turned the page to her own wedding portrait. She had her mother's classic bone structure and the same luxuriant halo of black hair. Back then it had not been tamed as it was now, and it had framed her face in a way that emphasized her incredible dark eyes. Miguel had been matinee-idol handsome, and the sparkle in his eyes as he regarded his new wife was a stark contrast to the melancholy look with which Molly was familiar.

After that there were mostly snapshots. The three sisters on the beach at Varadero. Two cou-

ples—Pilar and Miguel, Elena and Pedro—
seated in a dazzling nightclub in Havana. And to
Molly's surprise, there was one of Rosa, Michael's mother, on stage, standing at the micro-
phone, a big band behind her.

Then there were the children—building
sand castles on the beach, lined up in their finest
clothes on an Easter Sunday, at someone's first
communion. And finally there was Rosa with her
baby—Michael. Even though Rosa and the
American soldier with the Irish name had not
married, the family had not rejected her or her
illegitimate son.

"No pictures of your father?" Molly asked
quietly.

"None. If my mother ever had one, she de-
stroyed it. I've never seen him."

"Have you ever considered looking for
him?"

"For what?" He gestured around the room.
"This is my family. Miguel and Pedro, they were
my fathers."

When Pilar had turned the last page of the
album, a handful of photos tumbled loose.
Mostly there were more family snapshots, taken
when the children were perhaps a year or two
older than they had been in the pictures in the
album. But among the candid family photos,
there was one of a group of men wearing military fatigues. They were standing at the edge of a
field of sugarcane under a brilliant sun. Molly

immediately recognized Miguel and Pedro. She wasn't absolutely certain, but she thought the youngest man might have been Orestes León Paredes himself, his expression cocky, his stance arrogant. She glanced up at Michael.

"Paredes?"

It was Pilar who answered. "*Sí, es* Paredes."

Michael pointed to the fourth man in the snapshot. "That's José López, isn't it?"

Molly studied it more closely, looking for some sign of a resemblance to the shrunken, injured old man she had seen playing dominoes in the park. The man pictured was powerfully built and exuded vitality. Because she couldn't see it, she looked to Pilar for confirmation.

"*Sí,*" she said with an unmistakable trace of bitterness. "*Es José.*"

Molly exchanged a look with Michael. Obviously, he had caught the odd note in his aunt's voice as well. He asked her a question in Spanish. Rather than answering, she shoved the photos back into the album and snapped it shut. But when she started to stand, Michael gently held her in place.

"*Tía Pilar,*" he said firmly and repeated the question.

Molly understood only López's name and *aquí*. Apparently Michael was asking if the old man had been the one Miguel had seen the night before his disappearance. Had José López been *aquí*, here in this house?

Pilar's jaw set stubbornly, but a tear she couldn't control so easily escaped and tracked down her cheek. It was answer enough.

Michael squeezed her hand. "*Te quiero mucho*, Tía," he said. "I love you."

When they left, Pilar was rocking silently back and forth, the album clutched to her bosom.

CHAPTER
THIRTEEN

"Are you going to see Señor López about his meeting with Miguel?" Molly asked as they once again turned right on *Calle Ocho* off Twenty-seventh Avenue and headed west.

Michael shook his head. "Not yet. We're going to stop by La Carreta for lunch."

Molly regarded him in astonishment. "Isn't that some sort of betrayal, going to a restaurant other than Pedro's?"

"We're not going for the food. We're going for the conversation. I'm hoping we'll spot some of the same people who turned out for last night's protest. I'm sure that will be the hot topic of conversation over their *café Cubano* and *media noche* sandwiches. Maybe they'll be more forthcoming in the bright light of day."

Molly figured the odds of that were about

equal to the odds of her understanding half of the mostly Spanish conversation—slim. She wasn't sure she wanted to witness Michael's mounting frustration.

"That might be a good time for me to check in with Walt Hazelton at the paper and see if his sources in Cuba have anything to say about a stir in activity among the revolutionaries."

"It's probably a good time for you to call your ex-husband as well and make arrangements for Brian." At Molly's expression of distaste, he grinned. "Like taking a bitter medicine, *amiga,* you should get it over with."

"That's easy for you to say. You're not the one who's about to be the object of one of Hal's guilt-inducing tirades."

He regarded her intently. "If it bothers you so much, I could explain things to him."

Molly did rather like the image of Michael trying to talk reasonably with Hal DeWitt. They'd reacted like instinctive enemies on the past occasions when they'd met. It would be a real test of Michael's communication skills to see if he could get past all that predatory animosity, while keeping his own temper in check.

Regrettably, she also knew letting Michael make that call would be taking the coward's way out. "I'll call," she said resignedly.

To her amazement, when she got Hal on the line, the conversation actually went as smoothly as their earlier exchanges. The instant she explained the seriousness of the situation, he agreed that Brian should remain with him. He seemed especially pleased that she'd lived up to her promise to turn to him in an emergency.

"How are you two getting along?" Molly asked.

"We've hit a couple of rough patches," he admitted with what was for him amazing candor. He rarely wanted anyone to guess his failings. Hal DeWitt, partner in one of the most prestigious law firms in town, preferred that the world maintain its impression of him as a brilliant, successful attorney who was totally self-confident and untouched by the doubts that plagued ordinary men.

"What sort of rough patches? Over your new girlfriend?"

Hal's chuckle surprised her.

"So he told you about that?" he said.

"Is it something serious?"

"Not anymore."

"Meaning?"

"Seeing her treat Brian like an unwelcome intruder in my home woke me up."

"You don't suppose he did anything intentionally to antagonize her?" Molly asked, knowing that their son could be plenty devious when it suited his purposes.

"Not really. I think his presence was sufficient. I made it clear that his presence was welcome, and if she couldn't accept that, then her presence wasn't.''

''And?''

''She left.''

''You're okay with that?''

''Trust me, in retrospect I can see that it wasn't a great loss. I'm too old to be trying to keep up with some ambitious twenty-three-year-old law clerk anyway. Sooner or later I'd have begun to wonder if her interest in me was personal or professional.''

Molly had no comment on that. Well, to be perfectly honest, she had one, but it was best left unspoken if she intended to maintain this aura of amiability.

Hal hesitated, a rare occurrence for a man known in court for his quick-witted silver tongue. ''There is something I should probably tell you.''

''What?'' Molly asked with a sudden sense of impending doom. Broken arms and chicken pox came to mind. Naturally he'd want her off guard before dropping such a bombshell. ''What's wrong?''

''Nothing's wrong,'' he said irritably, then caught himself. ''It's just that having a kid around all the time, well, it can be damned difficult. Not that I haven't loved it, you understand,'' he added hurriedly.

Molly's mouth dropped open. Hearing such an admission from her extraordinarily competent, smug ex-husband was like unexpectedly wringing an honest response from a politician.

Hal chuckled again. "I've stunned you into silence, haven't I?"

"As a matter of fact, yes."

"The last few days have taught me a greater appreciation of what you've been coping with ever since we split. Juggling work and parenthood isn't quite the snap I expected it to be. I thought it was all a matter of organization. Boys don't always stick to the program, do they?"

"Almost never."

"You've done a good job with him, Molly," he said quietly. "I just wanted you to know that."

She couldn't think of a thing to say except, "Thank you."

"Be careful, okay?"

"Always. Tell Brian I love him and I'll try to call him tonight."

"Will do."

Michael came up behind her as she hung up. "Everything okay?"

"Amazingly enough, yes. He was actually decent about everything."

"That will make things easier between the two of you, yes?"

Molly nodded. "I feel as if this great weight has been lifted." She glanced up at Michael and said ruefully, "I wonder how long this accommodating mood will last."

"Just savor the moment," he suggested.

"Probably a good idea." She glanced beyond him toward the restaurant's main dining area. "Anyone here you were hoping to see?"

"There's one group of old men huddled in a corner. I've gotten the table closest to them."

"I'll be with you as soon as I've called Walt Hazelton. Order a sandwich for me, okay?"

Michael nodded. He turned to go, then came back. He reached up and cupped her face in his hands, his gaze steady on hers. "Thank you."

"For what?"

"For sticking with me through this."

She turned her head and pressed a kiss against his palm. "I wouldn't be anyplace else."

• • •

Walt Hazelton did have news from inside Cuba. Whether it was good or bad probably depended on the viewpoint. Molly couldn't quite decide what to think when he confirmed that in fact there had been reports of a handful of armed men arriving on the beaches along Cuba's north coast between Cojimar and Santa Cruz del Norte.

"One group was spotted and greeted with a hail of gunfire from Cuban soldiers. One man was killed and two others were wounded. A fourth escaped."

Molly's breath caught in her throat. "Any names?"

167

"Miguel García was not among them."

She released a pent-up sigh of relief. "Thank God. Were they the only ones?"

"There are several wild rumors circulating, including one saying an entire boatload of guns made it through and that even now guerrillas in the hills are arming themselves for a coup."

"Are you sure this is just a rumor?"

"No one I spoke with had seen these guns for themselves. It was always the friend of a cousin or some such who'd reported it. I wouldn't go to press with information that vague, but I heard it enough to suspect there may be some truth to it."

"But the bottom line is that Miguel could have been part of an attempted invasion and he could be inside Cuba now."

"It's possible," the reporter agreed.

He said it without much enthusiasm. Molly wondered about that. "What aren't you saying?"

"One thing doesn't make sense," he admitted.

"What's that?"

"Miguel took his boat out from here on Sunday morning. You went looking for him at midday and found the boat Sunday night, early Monday morning, right?"

"We found it an hour or so before sunset in Cuban waters. It was just before midnight when we got back. The explosion occurred just after midnight."

"According to the people I spoke with, those arrested said they had taken off from Key West."

"Perhaps Miguel was to meet up with them," Molly suggested, stretching to find a reasonable explanation. "That would explain why we found his boat adrift where we did and why his raft was missing."

"I don't think so."

"Why not?"

"Because this incident didn't take place until just before dawn this morning. I began getting calls as soon as I hit the office, calls from people I had spoken with just yesterday who had no news of this kind to report."

Molly wasn't willing quite yet to accept the implications of what he was saying. "Couldn't they have staged this to go in over a period of days? That way if one wave of guerrillas was picked up, others might still have a chance to get past the soldiers."

"It's possible, but everyone reliable I spoke with indicated that all those arriving safely had also arrived just today."

When Molly said nothing, Walt Hazelton said quietly, "I'm sorry. I know this isn't what you hoped to hear."

"At least it's something," she said finally. "We just have to figure out what it means."

When she told Michael what the foreign correspondent had learned, the color drained from his face.

"Miguel could still have gone in with them," Molly insisted, refusing to give up hope.

"And what has he done since Sunday? It is Tuesday now. Has he been floating around on a raft in Cuban waters waiting to rendezvous with his coconspirators?" He shook his head. "I don't like this. Something tells me Miguel was up to his neck in the planning for this, but that something went terribly wrong."

"You don't know that."

"But I know who would," he said with an air of grim determination.

He rose and walked over to the tableful of men across the aisle. They regarded him warily as he pulled up a chair and joined them.

Ignoring the food that had just been placed in front of her, Molly watched their faces, hoping she could detect something from their expressions since she couldn't understand their rapidly spoken words. All she heard were what sounded like vehement denials, accompanied by angry gestures. Michael's exasperated shouts rose above the uproar of the others, stunning them into furious, stubborn silence. He threw up his hands in a gesture of disgust and left them.

"What on earth did you say to them?" Molly asked when Michael stalked back to the table, picked up their check, and headed for the door. She had to race to catch up with him as he tossed a handful of bills onto the counter by the cash register.

"Michael?" she prodded him.

"I told them they were crazy old men if they believed they were any match for Castro's guns. I asked them if this was a plot by Paredes. Just like last night, they denied any knowledge of such a plot. Then they gave me a bunch of hogwash about the triumph of freedom against a godless regime."

He settled into the driver's seat of the car and rubbed his eyes before sliding his sunglasses into place. "I don't know how to deal with men like that," he said with a rare display of helplessness. "How can I make them trust me?"

"Not by calling them crazy old men," Molly replied.

He scowled at the rebuke. "Okay, it wasn't exactly tactful," he admitted, "but I'm out of patience and I may well be running out of time. If Miguel is still at sea on that damned raft without provisions, he could be dying while they talk ideals and politics."

Molly had one thought, but she knew instinctively that he was likely to resist it. "Michael, I really do think you must go to Señor López and talk to him."

"About what happened the night before Miguel disappeared?"

"About that, but more importantly about what it was like for them in Cuba when they were young. You saw them in that photo with Paredes. Those ties have never weakened. Paredes isn't likely to open up with so much at stake, but José López might. Maybe more than anyone else, he can make you understand what has gone on in your uncle's head and how he feels in his heart. I think this is something you need to hear."

As she'd expected, he dismissed the idea with a wave of his hand. "I've listened to Pedro. I've listened to all of them. What do you think the talk is at Sunday dinner three hours out of every four? Cuba in the old days. Havana in its glory. The faith that soon they will return. In every toast at every holiday, they repeat that next year's toast will be made in Cuba. No matter how long it's been, they say it with the same deep conviction each time."

Molly regarded him skeptically. "Do they really believe it? Or is it a habit they can't overcome because then they wouldn't know how to go on? They've talked for all these years, but have you listened?"

"I tell you it was impossible growing up in my family not to hear these things," he said impatiently.

"But have you really listened?" she repeated. "Perhaps it's time you discover what it means to be a Cuban in exile, especially to a man like Miguel García."

"I am a Cuban in exile."

She shook her head. "No, you're a Cuban who's grown up here, who has acclimated. If anything, you've rebelled against the dreams of Miguel and the others, just as many teenagers rebel against the expectations of their parents. You were educated here. Your friends are Anglos and African-Americans, as well as Cubans. You're a policeman, for goodness sakes, a part of the system. How much more acclimated could you be?"

When he started to argue, she held up a hand. "No, wait. Have you dreamed of going home, as they do? Are there things you lie awake nights remembering, longing for? Have you wanted to return to the Havana you remember, to walk its streets again? How much do you even remember about the first five years of your life, except for the sound of your grandmother's laughter?"

He sighed heavily. "Perhaps not enough," he admitted eventually. "Perhaps not enough."

CHAPTER
FOURTEEN

José López agreed to meet Michael and Molly that night at a performance by Cuban salsa queen Celia Cruz.

"I tried to talk him out of it," Michael told Molly when he'd hung up. "A club is no place for a quiet conversation. He said it would be an appropriate backdrop to what I need to hear, whatever that means."

"It probably means that they heard her perform in the old days in Havana. She really is quite something."

"You've heard her?" he asked, clearly amazed.

"At the *Calle Ocho* festival. She usually performs."

"You've been to the street festival?"

"Why are you so surprised? Hundreds of

thousands of people are jammed along Eighth Street every year to hear the music and pig out on the food."

"I'm just amazed that you were one of them."

She regarded him closely. "What about you?"

"I haven't been in years," he admitted. "Pedro talked me into helping with his food booth five or six years ago. There were too damned many people for me. I told him I'd pay somebody to help him out the next time."

"Another rebellion, perhaps?" she inquired dryly.

Michael frowned at her.

"Never mind. Speaking of Pedro, though, do you suppose we could stop by his restaurant and grab another sandwich?" she asked wistfully.

"We just ate."

"Maybe you ate. I barely got to the table before you dragged me out of the place."

"Sorry," he said, looking contrite. "I wasn't thinking." He drove the few blocks east and pulled into the parking lot beside Pedro's restaurant. Inside they found his uncle working the cash register, his expression somber. He gave them a distracted glance.

"Sit anywhere. I will join you when I can."

Although it was nearly two o'clock, the restaurant was still jammed. As they worked their way between the crowded tables, Molly spotted the two young rafters who'd been rescued the day before. She pointed them out to Michael. They were surrounded by people, clearly being treated as heroes. At the sight of Michael, though, they stood up and came forward. Molly was relieved to see that the color in their cheeks was more normal, even though their sunburn blisters had broken and still looked painful.

"Gracias, amigo," Ricardo said to Michael, a smile spreading across his face. "You were right. Your uncle has promised us work. We will work hard to repay his generosity."

Tony clasped Michael's hand. *"Sí,* we are very grateful," he said in his low, shy voice. "We will start tonight. That will be the beginning of our new life."

"I'm glad it worked out," Michael told them. "I see you have found some admirers."

"Everyone has been very good to us," Ricardo agreed with his ready grin.

Tony, however, regarded Michael worriedly. "There is so much to learn."

"You'll do fine," Molly told them. "You already speak English amazingly well. Soon you will fit right in with those your own age. By the time school starts in the fall, you'll already have friends."

"I am not so sure about school," Tony said. "Unless we can locate our uncle and he will take us in, we must work to live here."

"I'm sure my uncle will adjust your hours so

that you can attend classes," Michael said, dismissing their concerns. "You'll need an education if you are to get ahead in this country."

"Get ahead?" Ricardo repeated. *"No comprendo."*

"To be a success."

The teenager nodded emphatically. "Ah, yes, a success. The American success story, *sí*?" Both boys glanced down at their new jeans, fancy sneakers, and the teal-and-black T-shirts of the Florida Marlins baseball team. "With these gifts we look American already, yes?" Ricardo asked.

Molly nodded, thinking how desperately they wanted to be part of their new land while so many other exiles simply longed to go home again. Perhaps it was because the two teenagers understood better than anyone the harsh reality and desperation of life in Cuba today. Would they be able to find a common understanding with men like Miguel, or would their perceptions of Cuba be so at odds it would be as if they were speaking of different countries? Would the glamor of this new land wear off when they realized how hard they would have to work to attain what others had? Right now it all must seem a fantasy come true.

When Molly and Michael were alone at their table and the boys had left with their new friends, she looked at him. "How much do you recall about your first days here?"

A faraway look came over his face. "I was just

thinking about that, trying to identify with what those two boys must be feeling. I can't. I was so young. All I remember was crying when I realized my mother wasn't getting on that plane with me. I remember how alone I felt, even after I was living with Pedro and Elena and my cousins. A child at that age needs a mother more than freedom, I think."

His expression hardened, as if he'd been transported back in time. "That is why I had so much anger," he said quietly. "I threw incredible tantrums. Sometimes I would go to bed so hoarse from crying, there was no sound left in me. I was probably hoping they would send me back. I didn't understand that they couldn't. I was still angry when my mother finally came. I didn't speak to her for days. I refused to allow her close enough to hug me."

"That must have pained her deeply," Molly said, barely able to conceive of the heartbreak she would suffer if Brian ever shut her out so cruelly.

"I suppose it did. I was too caught up in my own hurt to think of hers."

"Perhaps you were afraid."

"Of what?"

"That she would leave you again."

A faint, rueful smile tugged at his lips. "Have I ever told you that you are very wise, *querida*?"

She grinned at him. "Not nearly enough. Do you suppose they would have heard any rumors of an impending attack by guerrillas from the U.S.?"

Michael shook his head. "They are boys. Like all teenage boys, I would guess their interest is in girls, not politics."

"Michael, they risked their lives to get to a new country. That doesn't sound like a couple of kids who are unaware of anything except their hormones. This wasn't some lark or an adventure."

"Are you so sure?"

"Sure? No, of course I can't swear to it. We'd have to ask them. But from everything I've seen about life in Cuba or in any other place that has suffered war or oppression of one sort or another, there is no such thing as a childhood or adolescence as we know it. You've seen the pictures of children from places like Bosnia or Ireland or the Middle East, children whose eyes tell you they are wise beyond their years. Based on that, I say Tony and Ricardo may still be in their teens, but they are men, not children."

"Perhaps they just wanted to live someplace where they could get a Big Mac and a milk shake."

"I guess we'll have to ask them directly when we see them again to see which of us is right." Pedro joined them then. He gave Molly a wan, dispirited smile as he sat down with his tiny cup of *café Cubano* and poured in a healthy dollop of sugar.

"*Qué pasa,* Tío?" Michael asked.

"I should be home with the family," Pedro complained. "But no one else can handle the register at this hour, and we could not remain closed forever."

"Elena and Mother are with Pilar. That's all she really needs right now."

"No, she needs Miguel. As I do. He is like my own brother after all these years."

"Did he come in here often?" Molly asked.

"I tried to persuade him to work for me, but he said his English was not good enough. Still, he would stop almost every afternoon for an hour or so. Even today, I keep glancing toward the door expecting him to appear."

"Was he usually alone?"

Pedro nodded. "He came alone, but always there were two or three friends at the counter. He would join them."

Michael nodded approvingly at Molly as he picked up on where she was headed with the questions. "Are any of those friends here now?" he asked, his gaze on the row of men seated at the Formica-topped counter at the front of the restaurant.

There were one or two men dressed in business suits, but most wore the more traditional *guayabera* shirts from the simplest style to those with tiny rows of fancy tucks. The men seemed to range in age from their sixties upward. One wrinkled old man appeared to be at least eighty, but he spoke with youthful passion and vehemence about whatever topic they were discussing.

Pedro scanned the row. "There is the political satirist Juan Cabrera on the end and next to him is Herman Gómez-Ortega. Juan and Miguel have known each other since the first year of school in Cuba. The Cabrera family lived only a little distance from Miguel's family. They both fought against Castro, but in different ways, Miguel with a gun, Juan with his words. The differences didn't matter in the end. Both were jailed."

"And Gómez-Ortega?"

"I know less about him." Pedro's gaze narrowed when he looked at the stoop-shouldered man bent over his cup of coffee.

Molly could see that the man's broad, weathered hands appeared unsteady as he lifted the cup to his mouth. "You don't like him, though, do you?" she asked.

"You are very perceptive," he said bitterly. "Herman has these crazy ideas. Perhaps it is because he spent too long in Castro's prisons. He has been here only since the Mariel boat lift in 1980. I suspect Castro was glad to get rid of him. He was a dissident, but he was also a troublemaker, a violent man."

"Did Miguel know him in Cuba, or did they meet here?" Michael asked.

181

"Perhaps it was in prison. I cannot say for sure."

"Could you suggest they join us?" Michael asked.

Pedro looked startled. "You wish to question them?"

Michael shrugged. "They are Miguel's friends. Perhaps he has taken them into his confidence or, if as you say Herman is a little *loco*, perhaps he knows of some crazy scheme to invade the island."

Pedro stood. "I will get them."

"Don't tell them I wish to question them. Say only that Miguel's nephew is here and would like to meet friends of his uncle."

Pedro nodded slowly. *"Comprendo."*

A few moments later the two men joined them. Herman walked with a limp, but his handshake was strong and his eyes were alert and cautious. Molly wondered at once if he was quite as crazy as Pedro thought. He struck her as shrewd. Juan Cabrera was the one with the faraway look in his eyes. Perhaps, though, he was merely dreaming of his next political article or satirical short story.

"I understand you both know my uncle well," Michael said.

"Miguel García is a strong man, a man of conscience," Herman said, settling into a chair with another cup of the strong Cuban coffee. "You should be proud of him."

"I am," Michael agreed. "Right now, though, I have to admit that I'm worried about him. When was the last time you spoke with him?"

"We had coffee here as usual on Saturday," Juan said.

"And what was his mood?"

"He talked of the fish he would catch in the morning. He said he would bring some by for my family, as always," Juan said.

Michael looked skeptical, but rather than cross-examining the old man as he might a witness to a crime, he merely turned his attention to Herman.

"And you? When did you last see him?"

"I was here on Saturday as well. It is something of a habit with us. We are three old men with little to occupy our time except talk and memories."

It sounded awfully disingenuous to Molly.

"And he spoke to you only of fishing?" Michael asked.

"As I recall," Herman said vaguely.

Michael attempted a casual disinterest, but Molly could see the tension in the set of his jaw. "Do either of you know Orestes León Paredes?" he asked.

"Everyone knows of Paredes," Herman said quickly. "Why do you ask?"

"Do you think it is possible that he would

have information about my uncle's disappear-ance?"

"He is a powerful man," Juan said thought-fully. "It is true he would have many contacts."

Herman's gaze had narrowed. "What is it you are really asking, *amigo*?"

Michael regarded him evenly. "I suppose I'm asking exactly how involved Miguel was in Paredes's organization. As his friends, you would know that, *sí*?"

Herman stood up. "This is not something I care to discuss with a stranger."

Juan objected at once. "Michael is not a stranger. He is the nephew of our friend."

Herman shrugged. "He is also a policeman. Is that not what Miguel told us? I have no use for the police, not in my country and not in this one. *Adiós*." He left the restaurant without glanc-ing either to the right or the left.

"Too many cruel years in prison," Juan ex-plained when he had gone. "I am sorry for his rudeness."

"It's okay," Molly said distractedly, her gaze fixed on Michael's expression. She recognized that look.

"Let's go, *amiga*," he said. He was polite enough to his uncle and to Juan Cabrera, but it was clear his attention was focused on the man who had just left them.

"Are we following Herman?" Molly asked as they got into the car.

Michael nodded, his gaze scanning the parking lot and the nearby curbside. "There," he said finally, and made a quick turn across traffic that had Molly clinging to the door and praying that the cars aimed straight at the passenger side had time enough to stop. She closed her eyes. Tires squealed and horns blew.

"You can open your eyes now," Michael said dryly.

"Don't you suppose that the ruckus you caused making that turn might have gotten Herman's attention?" she said, glancing ahead and hoping for a glimpse of the car they were tailing. She guessed it had to be the late-model white midsize Chevrolet.

Michael dismissed her concern. "My bet is he's too busy trying to get to Paredes to tell him about our chat. Where are those articles Ryan gave you?"

"In the backseat."

"Can you get to them?"

"As long as you don't arrest me for not wearing a seat belt."

"I'll close my eyes," he promised.

"Given the way you drive with them open, it probably wouldn't make that much difference," she observed. She snatched the papers from the back and snapped her seat belt into place. "Okay, what am I looking for?"

"Some mention of Herman in the articles about the organization."

Molly started skimming the printouts. Before she'd made it through the first two articles, Michael slammed on the brakes and muttered an expletive under his breath. For once it wasn't in Spanish, so she knew exactly how exasperated he was.

"What's wrong?"

"I don't get it."

She glanced out the window and spotted Herman at a pay phone in front of a convenience store. "So he's calling Paredes, rather than going to see him."

Michael shook his head. "I don't think so."

"Why not?"

"Because it looks to me like he's holding a long distance calling card in his hand."

"What does that mean? Do you think he's an infiltrator working for the government?"

"Your imagination is working overtime, *amiga*. Besides, a government operative would have memorized the number."

"Maybe he's just making a business call that has absolutely nothing to do with this."

"Maybe," he agreed, but he sounded doubtful.

"I could go into the store and try to catch some of his conversation." She already had her hand on the door.

"Forget it. It would tip him that we're following him."

"The man looked straight through me the

whole time we were sitting there. I doubt he'd even recognize me."

"Don't kid yourself. He could probably give you a detailed description of every single person seated near us in that restaurant. I watched him. He missed nothing."

Molly recalled her own first impression of his alertness. Even though he appeared to have ignored her, Michael was probably right about his generally sharp observance of both her and his surroundings. "So what do we do now?"

"When he gets off that phone and into his car, you go over and take down the number. Then call the operator and say you were disconnected on a long distance call and ask if she can reconnect."

"He made the call. Won't she think it's odd that I can't tell her what number I made that call to?"

"Bluff. Do the best you can. At the very least, we'll have this number and perhaps the long distance carrier he used. Perhaps later we can trace the call, if it becomes necessary."

"How will we know the carrier?"

"Because I counted the numbers he dialed. He didn't need an extra access number to reach his carrier, so whatever company the phone is linked to is his carrier. It probably says on the information card on the front of the phone."

Molly kept her awe at his observation skills to

herself. "Can I assume that while I'm on the phone, you won't be waiting here patiently?"

"That's right. I'll be following him. If I'm not back in fifteen minutes, take a cab back to Pedro's and I'll pick you up there." He glanced toward the pay phone. "Okay, this is it. Be careful. Don't let him see you."

"Would you like me to lie down on the sidewalk until he's passed by?"

Apparently he missed her sarcasm, because he nodded without taking his eyes off his quarry. "Good idea."

Molly climbed out of the car and hunkered down, inching her way to the van parked two spaces up. Standing behind that, she was sufficiently out of view from the street, but could see the exit from the convenience store lot. She watched as Herman pulled out of the lot and headed west, just as Michael had anticipated. Michael waited until there were several cars in between, then pulled away from the curb and into traffic a few cars behind him.

When they were out of sight, Molly strolled across the street to the pay phone. Unfortunately, all that caution had left the phone unattended. Someone else had taken advantage of the opportunity to grab it. Molly paced impatiently behind the woman, who seemed in no hurry to conclude her astonishingly graphic tête-à-tête. Must have been a lover, Molly decided. Women almost never sneaked out to a pay phone to make calls like that to their husbands, not after the first year of marriage anyway. When the woman finally did hang up, she didn't even spare Molly a glance. Apparently she wasn't the least bit concerned about having the details of her love life overheard.

Molly jotted down the number on the phone, saw that it was an AT&T hookup, then punched the "0" to get the operator. "Hi, I don't know if this is possible, but I'm at a pay phone and I placed a call to someone a few minutes ago. I've managed to lose the piece of paper the number was written on. It's probably in my purse, but I sure can't find it. Isn't it amazing how things can get swallowed up in a woman's handbag? Anyway, we were cut off in the middle of our conversation and I have no idea how to reach him."

She took a hint from the conversation she'd just overheard and threw herself on the operator's mercy. "It's really important. It's this guy. I'm really crazy about him, but I'm beginning to think he's married. I think he had me call him at a pay phone. Can you check for me or maybe get him back on the line? If it was a pay phone or something, I'll know he's cheating on a wife or girlfriend."

She was rather proud of the barrage of words. She waited to see if they'd been effective.

"Hon, I sympathize, but I can't do that."

"You mean because it's illegal?"

"You'd have to have a real emergency and even then I don't have the equipment to do it. Somebody'd have to authorize the check on the outgoing calls from your pay phone."

Molly sighed dramatically. "Oh, well, it was worth a shot." She was ready to hang up, but the operator wasn't through.

"Next time you talk to this guy, hon, you tell him you want to know how to reach him and if he won't tell you, you dump him. Don't waste your time, okay?"

Molly decided the operator had read too many pop psychology books or maybe she'd just seen too many weird episodes of Geraldo and hated to think of anyone getting caught up in some bizarre romantic triangle. "Thanks, I'll do that," Molly promised.

Just as she hung up, she spotted Michael's car turning into the lot.

"What did you get?" he asked.

"Advice," she said with disgust. "How about you?"

"Lost. He drove into Coral Gables and the next thing I knew, he'd taken a couple of fast turns and disappeared. The way those streets twist around in there, I was lucky to get back out again. I don't know where the hell I was. I wish they'd put their street signs up on poles where you can read them like any other civilized place."

"They think they're more civilized right

where they are, discreetly placed at curb height." She couldn't resist taking a poke at his tailing skills. "So the bottom line is you lost Herman, huh?"

He shrugged. "Probably doesn't matter, since he clearly wasn't heading to see Paredes after all."

"You'll never know that for sure, unless we drive out there and check. Could be Herman just knows his way around the Gables."

Michael looked doubtful, but he turned the car west. It was a good thing he did, too. They arrived in front of Paredes's house along with three squad cars and an ambulance.

"What's going on?" Michael demanded of the first cop he saw.

"Somebody tried to murder the guy who lives here, blasted the hell out of the house with some kind of automatic weapon."

"Is he okay?"

"The lucky son of a bitch wasn't even home. From what the neighbors say, he moved out yesterday."

CHAPTER
FIFTEEN

With police everywhere, the neighbors—mostly women with small children—began slowly emerging from their houses. While Michael continued to talk to the investigating officers, Molly wandered over to a cluster of housewives, all dressed in shorts and tank tops regardless of their size. On one or two, the choice was unfortunate.

Several of the young women were clutching babies in their arms. She observed them for several minutes, trying to pick out the one who was most talkative. The unofficial spokesperson appeared to be in her late twenties, slightly older than the others. Her two children were toddlers, one of whom was clinging to Mommy's leg and whining. The women appeared oblivious to the noise.

Molly nodded at several of the women, hoping she appeared to be a new neighbor, rather than someone there on official business. Actually, given her lack of official status, she supposed it wasn't exactly a stretch to be considered just another nosy passerby. "What happened? I saw all the police and walked over."

As she'd expected, it was the oldest of the women who replied. "I was in the back with the kids and all of a sudden I heard these shots. I looked around, didn't see anyone, so I dragged the kids inside. That's when I finally peeked out the window and saw this car sitting in front of the house over there. Some guy was just blasting away. Scared the hell out of me. I dialed nine-one-one and kept the kids on the floor in the back of the house."

"Has anything like this ever happened around here before?" Molly asked.

"Good God, no. I'd have made my husband move, if it had," she said.

Several other heads nodded in agreement.

"I'm Molly DeWitt, by the way. I don't know a soul around here yet. Who lives there?" she asked.

The women were either cautious enough or distracted enough not to bother offering their own names. Molly's chatty source, however, didn't hesitate over her reply. Like a lot of people who've just gone through a crisis, she was anxious to share the experience. Fortunately she didn't seem suspicious at all of Molly's interest.

"The people only moved in a few months ago," she told Molly. "They stayed to themselves. I hardly ever saw the wife. We went by once to ask her if she wanted to take her kids to the park with us, but she refused. We didn't try again. She was a real pretty woman, way too young for him. I got the feeling that husband of hers kept her on a pretty tight leash. And those dogs of his . . ." She shuddered. "I used to wonder what would happen if they ever got loose. We all told our kids to stay as far away from there as possible."

Having had a close encounter with the dogs herself, Molly understood their concern. "Did they have a lot of visitors? Had you ever seen the guy who shot at the place today before?"

"I suppose it's possible he's been around. The guy seemed to have friends here at all hours. We thought maybe he was into drugs or something. I mean, that's what I told my husband the very first week they lived there, what with all the coming and going. In fact, when I first heard all the gunfire, I thought maybe it was the start of one of those cocaine lab explosions I've seen on the news."

"And you'd never reported your suspicions to the police?"

"Hey, around here we try to mind our own business. It's safer that way. Besides, none of us ever really saw anything. It wasn't like he was collecting money in the street."

Molly nodded. "I see what you mean. Just think how you'd feel if you turned someone in and the only thing he was guilty of was keeping late hours. So," she added nonchalantly, "what kind of car was this guy driving today?"

The woman shrugged. "Are you kidding me? I can't tell a Jeep from a Jaguar. Made my husband put a bright yellow sunflower on our antenna so I could find our car in the parking lot at the mall."

"I think it might have been a Chevy," a young Hispanic woman offered hesitantly. "My brother has a car that looks exactly like it, only his is that pretty bright blue color and this one was white."

A white Chevrolet, Molly thought triumphantly. Exactly like the one Herman Gómez-Ortega had been driving when they followed him from Pedro's restaurant.

She shook her head sorrowfully. "Jeez, it's getting so no place is safe anymore, isn't it? I think I'll go talk to the cops and see if they think this was some random thing or a hit."

One of the younger mothers shivered and held her baby a little tighter. "You think it could have been random, like somebody who might come back to the neighborhood?"

Molly immediately felt guilty. "No. I mean it

almost has to be someone who was after the people who lived in that house, don't you think?''

"I wonder if that was why they moved out?''
another of the women speculated. "Because they
knew someone was after them?''

"All I can say is it's lucky for them they did,''
Molly's primary source observed. "This time of
day, the kids were usually inside taking a nap in
the front bedroom and the woman was watching
some soap opera on TV right by that window
that got blasted out.''

This time Molly shuddered right along with
them. She glanced toward Michael and wondered if he'd found out about the car. She
doubted it. All the witnesses were women and all
of them were over here. Obviously the police
were too busy inside to worry about chatting
with the neighbors yet. She decided it was time
to take her piece of information and go.

"I'll let you know if I find out anything from
the police,'' she said, and walked back across the
street.

When she finally got Michael's attention, he
joined her beside her car. "I think it's time to
run a Department of Motor Vehicles check on
Herman,'' she suggested.

He grinned. "Oh, you do, do you? Who died
and left you in charge of a police investigation?''

She frowned at the sarcasm. "It just occurred
to me that you might want to see where he lives
and what kind of car he drives.''

"I know what kind of car he drives. I was following him, remember?"

"Oh, I'd be willing to bet that the car he was in today was not his," she said, advancing a theory that had struck her as she crossed the street.

His gaze narrowed. "Why the hell would you say that?"

"Would you drive your own car if you intended to try to murder someone in broad daylight?"

He regarded her in stunned amazement. "What the hell did those women tell you?"

"Not much," she said modestly. "They did describe the car of the assailant as being a white Chevrolet. Isn't that the kind of car we were tailing?"

Michael's approving expression lasted for half a heartbeat, before he looked more puzzled than ever. "But why would Gómez-Ortega want to kill Paredes? I thought they were coconspirators."

"Guess not," Molly said smugly.

"Unless he knew that Paredes had moved out, knew it was safe to blast away, and just wanted to create a diversion from whatever is really going on," Michael said thoughtfully.

Molly sighed. "Damn, you've done it again."

"Done what?"

"Turned all devious on me, just when I had things figured out all logically."

"It's not my deviousness you need to worry

about, *amiga*. We're trying to think like the bad guys."

"That's what worries me," she said. "You do it so well. It's bound to rub off."

Michael called police headquarters and had Felipe run the DMV check on Gómez-Ortega. When Felipe called back as they were driving away from the scene, he confirmed Molly's guess. Gómez-Ortega didn't own a white Chevy or anything that might have been mistaken for one. He had, however, leased one from a small rental car agency on South Dixie Highway, an independent company that was less likely to ask questions or keep records. Unfortunately for Herman, the trail was still hot when Felipe called.

"Are we going to question him?" Molly asked hopefully.

"Nope. Felipe's offered to have a chat with him. You and I are going to get all dressed up and meet José López."

"But we're not meeting him until nine o'clock," Molly protested.

"With the distractions I have in mind, *amiga*, it will take you that long to get ready."

● ● ●

The salsa beat was seductive. Celia Cruz might be an aging songstress, but she knew exactly how to capture her audience with the passion and soul of her music. People around Molly, Michael, and

José López were on their feet, swaying to the provocative rhythm. Molly would have been totally caught up in it herself if it hadn't been for Michael sitting there impatiently tapping a silver spoon on the table. She knew it was impatience, because he wasn't even close to the music's beat.

Señor Lopez, in contrast, couldn't have been happier. In fact, he hadn't looked this pleased when he'd won the dominoes game the day before. His expression was dreamy, as if Celia Cruz's music had reached his soul and transported him back to late-night Havana.

When the set finally ended, the old man dragged his attention from the stage down front in the crowded supper club to Michael. "Your mother was even better," he said. "She sang like a lark. Everyone who heard fell a little in love with her."

Michael appeared startled. "I don't recall ever hearing her sing."

"Perhaps not. After she fell in love and your father left her, I think the romance went out of her soul."

Molly sensed Michael tensing beside her. She caught a fleeting glimpse of guilt, as if Rosa Huerta's loss of romance were his responsibility. How often, she wondered, had he blamed himself just for being born?

"It is Miguel I want to talk about," Michael said stiffly. "Tell me what you recall of my uncle."

"Miguel García was a dreamer. When Fidel began to talk of a better future for the masses, Miguel was one of the first we knew to embrace his words. He had seen firsthand the struggles of so many of our people to rise above poverty. He dreamed that a classless society was possible."

"What happened to change his mind?"

"Like so many of us, he quickly grew disenchanted when he saw the military force that would be used to make change. It grew worse when he saw that Fidel sought power almost as greedily as he sought change, and worse yet when he saw land and businesses seized indiscriminately. Then, when he saw brothers fighting against brothers, much as they did in this country's Civil War, he rebelled. As he had been among the first to join Fidel's cause, he was also among the first to seek his overthrow. It was only by the grace of Almighty God that he escaped with his life. He brought that passionate hatred for Fidel to this country. He holds himself partly accountable for all that went wrong in Cuba. All these years he has seethed with the need to make things right."

Michael seemed to be struggling to understand such powerful emotions. "He would do anything, then?"

"Anything," the old man agreed.

"Including taking part in a foolhardy invasion even less likely to be successful than the Bay of Pigs?"

"Ideals are not something you give up in the face of hardship. The odds would not have deterred him, not if there were even the slimmest margin of hope."

"Has Paredes staged such an attack?" Michael asked, though he looked no more hopeful of a straightforward response now than before.

"This is not for me to say. You have asked him this, yes? What did he say?"

"He denied knowledge of it." Michael pinned the old man with a piercing gaze. "But he would deny it, even if it were true, wouldn't he? He would deny it because he knows it is a violation of the Neutrality Act to stage a paramilitary attack on Cuba from American soil."

As she listened, Molly had a sudden terrifying thought. "Señor, how would Paredes and the others feel about one of their people working for the newspaper they regard with such hatred?"

For the first time since they'd sat down at the table, José López looked as uneasy as he had on the first day they'd questioned him. Michael clearly recognized that uneasiness.

"Well, Señor?" he prodded.

"There are some who might view it as traitorous. But," he added quickly, "they are extremists, and there are few of them."

"It only takes one," Michael said quietly. He leveled another look at López. "I want names of those who might have considered my uncle such a traitor. Would Paredes himself have felt that way?"

Señor López looked pale, even in the restaurant's dim light. "I have heard him say such things, yes."

"But he would not personally have acted on his opinion, would he?" Molly asked.

The old man shook his head. "No, but there are always those who will do anything to please a leader such as Paredes. These men are anxious for violence. They see spies and traitors everywhere."

Michael covered the old man's hand. "Names, Señor. For the sake of your good friend, I want you to give me names."

López seemed to struggle with his conscience. "I cannot," he said sorrowfully. "I am making my own inquiries, but I cannot help you with yours."

Michael regarded him shrewdly. "Perhaps your own name should be on that list," he suggested.

A tear spilled down José López's cheek. "Miguel was my friend," he said softly. "Again and again I told him he was embracing the enemy with that damnable job of his, but he would not hear it. He said putting food on his family's table did not constitute a betrayal of the cause."

He lifted his watery gaze to meet Michael's. "But I did not harm him," he said emphatically. "I could no more have harmed Miguel than taken a gun to my own head. No, my friend, if you think I am capable of that, you are a fool and you are wasting precious time."

"It is not I who waste it, but you," Michael said accusingly.

"I am doing what I can." He reached for his crutches then and hobbled away from the table, his shoulders stiff with pride and anger.

Molly exchanged a glance with Michael. "Do you think he was telling the truth?"

"About not being involved in my uncle's disappearance? Probably. About not knowing who was involved? No. I believe he knows or suspects."

"Why wouldn't he tell you, then?"

"And betray the goddamned cause?" Michael said angrily. "Can't you see that he would go to his death first?"

"It is a code of honor among them," Molly reminded him.

"And under other circumstances, perhaps I could admire it. With my uncle's life at stake, *amiga,* I cannot afford to."

CHAPTER
SIXTEEN

When they got back to Michael's townhouse, Molly was the one who spotted the blinking light on his answering machine. Five messages.

"Michael, it's Jorge Martinez," began the first disembodied voice. "I just wanted to let you know we didn't pick up anyone in the Straits today, just a couple of empty rafts, the makeshift kind, not anything Miguel would have been on. Sorry, *amigo*. I will go up again myself tomorrow. Call if you've had any word."

"Damn," Michael muttered. "I should have been out there when they came in."

"For what? The bad news? You're doing your part to break the case, while they do theirs. They understand that."

"I suppose," he said as the second message began.

"O'Hara, it's Felipe. Call me at headquarters when you get in. I've had a chat with Herman. He claims to have no idea where you got the information that he had anything to do with the attack on Paredes's home. He swears he left your uncle's restaurant, stopped to make a call, then cut through Coral Gables to take the car back to the rental agency on Dixie Highway. I can't prove otherwise, because there's no exact time listed for his check-in. Ken said he'd go down and do a search of the car for some trace of gunpowder or shell casings if you want him to. Let me know how you want me to follow up. Should I turn this over to the investigating officers on the Paredes incident?"

Michael sank into a chair and held his head. "Damn, we're drawing blanks everywhere."

The next message began. "Michael, this is Pedro. Call Pilar's when you get in. I am worried about her. She has gone to her bed and won't speak to anyone."

"Terrific," he muttered, hitting the off button on the machine before it could play the remaining messages. "That's just great. Now Pilar is going to have a breakdown."

Molly stood behind him and massaged his shoulders. "Bed is probably the best place for her. She hasn't rested since this all began."

"She's not resting, dammit. She's sinking into a depression."

"Then we'll just have to come up with good news to snap her out of it."

Michael reached up and put a hand over hers. "I appreciate your optimism, *amiga*, but I think it is misguided."

Molly turned the answering machine back on. "There are two more messages. Either one of them could be the break we need."

The first, however, was a call from Bianca. Molly bristled when she heard the name. Bianca was the woman with whom Michael had been living when Molly had first met him.

"I am so worried about you," she said in a low, seductive voice that set Molly's teeth on edge. It didn't seem to matter that she was here and the other woman was not.

"Please call me and tell me what I can do to help," the message continued. "I spoke with your mother today and she said you are exhausted. *Por favor, mi amor*, let me do something."

Molly stopped the tape, her gaze pinned on Michael's face. It betrayed no emotion at the sound of his old lover's voice. "Do you want to call her?"

He seemed startled by the question. "For what? It is over between us."

"This is a crisis. Obviously she would like to help."

"And my calling would send her the wrong message. It is best to leave things as they are."

He touched Molly's cheek. "Do not looked so worried, *amiga*, you have nothing to fear from Bianca."

"I wasn't worried."

His lips curved slightly. "If you say so."

Because it was not a statement she cared to examine any more closely, Molly punched the button to listen to the last message. It was from Walt Hazelton for her.

"I'll be at the paper until midnight or one. Call me." There was a sense of urgency in his voice.

"See, I told you that a break was just around the corner," she said triumphantly. "I'll bet he's learned something."

"Or he's trying to pick your brain."

"For what?"

"To discover what we've learned today."

"Then he'll be disappointed, won't he?"

When she got the correspondent on the line, he said, "I just wanted to be sure you'd heard about what happened out at Paredes's place this afternoon."

Offer of information or sneaky ploy? She supposed the reporter's statement might indicate there was some truth to Michael's cynical suggestion. Molly was willing to play along for the moment. "I was out there right after it happened."

"Then you know he'd moved out," he said.

"Yes. Any idea where he is?"

"I've been making calls all afternoon. He's disappeared without a trace. My sources have clammed up completely. My sense is that something big is about to break."

"Like what? An attempted overthrow of Castro?"

"Could be that or could be another Mariel situation, when the floodgates open. Washington's been working on an emergency plan to cope with another influx of exiles from Cuba or Haiti for months now. If O'Hara picks up anything on Paredes's whereabouts, will you let me know?"

"I'll do my best," Molly said, resigned to the fact that Hazelton knew no more than she did at this point. She was ready to hang up when it occurred to her that the correspondent could save her a lot of time digging into Herman Gómez-Ortega's background. She mentioned his name.

"Why do you ask?"

At a warning look from Michael, she hedged her answer. "Turns out he and Miguel were friends. He didn't particularly strike me as the friendly type."

"He's a mean son of a bitch, actually. He and Paredes are like two peas in a pod, though Herman has more of a reputation for violence. He's been head of military operations for the Paredes organization, though he would deny that. There was talk for a while that he was also the mastermind behind some bombing incidents targeting Cuban diplomats. People in Washington keep a very close eye on him. To hear him tell it, though, he is nothing more than a simple businessman, trying to live out his remaining years in peace.''

"Thanks, Walt." When she'd hung up, Molly relayed what he'd said to Michael.

"A simple businessman? Sure doesn't sound like the man who took an assault weapon to Paredes's house today, does it?" he said. "I'll give Felipe a call and fill him in."

Molly paced while Michael was on the phone. His expression turned more and more grim as the mostly one-sided conversation went on. Since she had no idea what Felipe was saying, she had to assume it was more bad news.

"Well?" she asked when he'd hung up.

"Ken went by on his way home and took a look at the rental car. He couldn't find so much as a trace of evidence that it had been used in that shooting incident. He thinks we should turn it over to the investigating officers and let them do a more thorough check, but he doubts they'll come up with any more than he did. He said it looked to him like the damn thing had been gone over by a detail crew. The carpet had been shampooed, the seats cleaned, the whole nine yards."

"Which seems like a lot of trouble to go to

before returning a rental car, unless a kid threw up all over the upholstery," Molly commented.

"Or unless someone is trying to cover up something," he added. "Unfortunately, I can't think of a court anywhere who'd take clean carpet and upholstery as evidence of a crime."

• • •

Molly awoke in the morning to the sound of glass breaking and a string of expletives in English and Spanish that would have made a sailor blush. She grabbed one of Michael's shirts and buttoned it as she ran down the stairs.

"What on earth?" she said as she skidded to a stop at the kitchen door. The radio was on the floor in pieces, along with a shattered coffee cup and bits of a juice glass. Coffee and orange juice were splattered all over the wall and the carpet. Michael was sitting down, staring at the mess, a dazed expression on his face. He looked as if he weren't quite sure how it had happened.

Molly picked her way through the shards of glass and hunkered down in front of him, her hands on his thighs. "What happened? What did you hear on the radio?"

"What makes you think I heard something on the radio?"

She gestured toward the bits of plastic, batteries and knobs scattered every which way. "People have a way of taking out their frustrations over the message on the messenger."

He sighed. "True. If Díaz-Nuñez had been in the vicinity, I might very well have treated him the exact same way."

"Ah, I see. And what did our favorite newscaster have to say this morning?"

"To hear him tell it, Paredes's organization is a hotbed of traitors and spies who have infiltrated at Castro's behest. Death, he says, is not good enough for those who commit these crimes against the Cuban patriots. What happened to Miguel García, he says, was only a warning to the others."

Molly regarded him in shock. "Luis Díaz-Nuñez called your uncle a traitor? Why?"

"Do you think he felt a need to explain?" he said bitterly. "It also sounds to me as if he believes he is dead." His eyes blazed with fury as he reached for the phone.

"You aren't calling him?" Molly said.

"Why not? I will not have him slander my family in this way."

"Do you honestly think what you say will matter to a man like Díaz-Nuñez?"

"But my uncle should be defended."

"And in due time, he will be. For now, though, shouldn't you be thinking of Pilar? What will she think when she hears on the radio any hint that Miguel might be dead?"

"Dear God, I never thought of that. Let's go. We have to get over there."

When they arrived at the house, already

there were a handful of protesters marching on the front lawn, people spurred on by the rhetoric of Díaz-Nuñez. Molly wondered if she would be able to get Michael to pass them by without his responding to the jeers. A brawl would do nothing to help Pilar, though at the moment it might help Michael to release his pent-up outrage. Come to think of it, she wouldn't mind belting a few of them herself. She recognized them from earlier visits. These same people had been by to express their sympathy and concern for a man they had respected. Now Díaz-Nuñez and his unexplained labeling of Miguel as a traitor had turned them against their friend.

Michael displayed admirable restraint as he passed by. Inside, they found Pilar being comforted by Michael's mother and Tía Elena. Pedro was trying to keep Michael's cousins from going outside to run off the band of protesters.

"They will only come back," he told them.

"But they are telling lies about Miguel. They say he has betrayed Cuba. He would never do that. How can they turn on him this way?" one of the youngest cousins asked.

"It is easy to stir up old fears," Pedro told them. "Logic and truth are no match for the rhetoric of hatred, given in the guise of patriotism. We know how deeply Miguel believed in Cuba. We know that the words spoken on the radio are lies, that Díaz-Nuñez has offered no facts, just allegations, but to say that we know those things will not be enough. Time will prove us right.''

The younger men all looked to Michael. "Do you agree that we should do nothing?''

Michael glanced out the window, his jaw tense with anger. Finally he nodded with obvious reluctance. "Tío Pedro is right. We will not change their minds. It is more important that we keep Pilar's spirits high and that I find Miguel. We cannot lose our focus over this.''

When Michael went to speak quietly with his aunt, Pedro pulled Molly aside. "I am worried about him. I can see his anger and his pain, but he keeps it inside.''

"He is strong," Molly reassured him. "Stronger than any of us. And he is motivated by love for his uncle.''

"You will see that he rests, that he does not drive himself too hard?''

"I will try," she promised. "But Michael knows his own limits, or thinks he does. I have little influence.''

Pedro smiled wearily. "You have more than you know, Molly. He cares for you a great deal, I believe. And right now he needs you, whether he admits that to you or not.''

The concept of Michael O'Hara's needing anyone was something Michael himself would have rejected out of hand, but Molly believed in her heart that Tío Pedro was right. The tough, stubborn cop needed someone he could rely on, and she intended to do everything in her power to be that person, not just now, but in the future as well.

She gave Tío Pedro a hug. "I'll watch out for him. I promise."

"Then perhaps you'd better hurry," he said dryly. "He appears to be sneaking out the front door without you."

Molly whirled around just in time to see Michael closing the door behind him. "Michael O'Hara," she shouted as she took off after him. "Don't you dare try to leave me behind."

The rare sound of laughter followed her out the door. She caught up with Michael at his car. "Exactly what did you think you were doing?" she demanded.

"Leaving."

"Without me?"

He pressed his hand to her cheek. "*Amiga,* I knew you would not be far behind."

"You counted on me following?"

"Yes."

"Then why not just tell me it was time to go?"

"Because then I would have had to explain to everyone that we are going to see Díaz-Nuñez and I knew that such an announcement would create a furor. Pedro would have wished to come along. My cousins would have insisted on joining us. Soon we would have had a goddamned parade."

"Haven't you ever heard the expression 'there's strength in numbers'?"

"Yes, but just this once I believe I can make my point more effectively alone. I do not want the others around when I tear that man limb from limb."

"You will not do that," Molly said.

He regarded her with obvious skepticism. "Oh? How can you be so certain?"

"Because you are a policeman and, for better or worse, you believe in the judicial system."

"Then what would you suggest I do to deal with the man who slandered my uncle and brought shame upon my family?"

Molly grinned. "Let me tear him limb from limb."

Michael's burst of laughter momentarily silenced the ragtag band of protesters on the lawn. He pulled Molly into his arms and held her tightly. "Ah, *querida*, have I mentioned that I adore you?"

"No, but I'm glad to hear it."

"Oh?"

"It makes it so much nicer, since I adore you."

CHAPTER
SEVENTEEN

En route to the radio station, Molly tried to keep Michael focused on a plan of attack that did not involve bloodshed.

"It's possible that Díaz-Nuñez is being fed false information about Miguel. With his strong political sentiments, he would be an easy pawn if someone wanted to start a conspiracy of lies. The merest hint that someone is a traitor or a spy would bring him out swinging. He doesn't strike me as someone who requires facts before going on the air."

Michael considered her suggestion thoughtfully. "You could be right. But why would someone do that?"

"To stir up trouble, perhaps. To divert attention from some other scheme. That will become clearer when you find out who his source is, don't you think?''

"I suppose.''

"So you'll ask questions about where he got his information, right? You'll stay calm and listen to the answers?''

"You ask a lot of a man, *amiga.*''

"Yes,'' she agreed cheerfully. "But I know you can easily live up to my expectations.''

"And if I do not, if I suddenly feel the need to put my fist down the man's throat?''

"Then I'll forgive you,'' she said generously.

He looked at her. The mirrored sunglasses kept her from detecting the emotion in his eyes, but she guessed she would find tolerant amusement there.

"I do not need your permission or your forgiveness,'' he pointed out.

"Of course not,'' she responded dutifully.

He sighed at the too-ready agreement. "I'll do my best not to disappoint you.''

"I never doubted it.''

Molly had not counted on the fact that she would be the one who wanted very badly to put a fist down the newscaster's throat. She took one look into those smug eyes and felt her civilized veneer being stripped away. Michael, however, suddenly seemed icily calm. If anything, it was more frightening than his hotheaded anger.

"In your office,'' he said to Díaz-Nuñez when they came face-to-face during a commercial break. The newscaster had stepped into the hallway outside the studio from which he'd been broadcasting.

"I have another hour left on the air," Díaz-Nuñez protested.

"Someone will cover for you, I'm sure." Michael regarded him speculatively. "Or we could play our discussion over the airwaves. Would you prefer that?"

"That will not be necessary," he replied stiffly. "I will make arrangements."

Moments later they heard Latin music pouring from the speakers that lined the hallway. Díaz-Nuñez joined them again, then preceded them into his office. He settled himself behind his desk and reached for one of his cigars.

"I have questions," Michael informed him. "Quite a lot of them, as a matter of fact."

"And if I am not inclined to answer?"

"Then perhaps you would prefer to answer them at police headquarters," Michael said indifferently. "It doesn't matter to me."

"This is an official interrogation, then?"

"Official enough, but I am not charging you with my uncle's death just yet," he said with a magnanimous air.

There was a fleeting hint of panic in Díaz-Nuñez's eyes before he banked it. "Why would you think I know anything of Miguel García's death?"

"Because you are the only one to say he is

dead," Michael replied. "The police have not said it. The Coast Guard has not said it. The rescuers flying over the Florida Straits have not said it. So, then, I have to ask how you would know this with such certainty, if you are not involved."

"I don't know anything," Díaz-Nuñez protested. "He disappeared days ago. There has been no trace. I assume he is dead."

He couldn't have said anything that would infuriate Michael more. Molly watched the color rise in his cheeks, saw his hands clench until the knuckles turned white.

"And you broadcast this assumption on the air as fact?" Michael said in a low, furious voice. "You dare to distress my aunt in this way, based on assumptions, on guesswork? What sort of journalist are you?"

The newscaster took the criticism without batting an eye. "I rely on a combination of facts, sources, and instincts."

Visibly fighting to bring his temper in check, Michael stood up, placed his hands on the desk, and leaned forward until he was only inches from the other man's face. "And which of those told you my uncle was a traitor?"

Díaz-Nuñez nervously twisted the cigar in his hands. He refused to lift his eyes to meet Michael's gaze. "For that I had a source," he swore. "A most reliable source."

Seconds ticked by in silence. The newscaster finally looked up and regarded Michael warily, as did Molly. She wasn't sure what he would do in the face of such a bold claim of attribution.

"Who?" he demanded finally. "Who told you this?"

"I cannot reveal that. A journalist must protect his sources," Díaz-Nuñez said piously. "Surely you can understand that."

Michael's expression turned lethal. "I understand that if you do not give me a name, then I must assume that you alone are responsible for the slander. And that it will be you I must deal with."

Suddenly Díaz-Nuñez went on the attack, lifting himself from his chair and leaning toward Michael, who then took a step back. "Why do you defend a man who would betray his brothers?" he asked hotly. "Are you a traitor as well, *O'Hara?*"

He said the name as disparagingly as he could, emphasizing the fact that it was not Hispanic. There was no question Michael understood the intended insult.

Michael snagged a handful of the newscaster's perfectly pressed silk-blend shirt and hauled him halfway across the fancy mahogany desk, scattering papers in his wake. "Miguel García is a Cuban patriot. I would stake my life on that. If you have evidence to the contrary, if you have a source who says otherwise, then produce it. Do not be a coward standing behind a false claim of journalistic ethics."

Molly had managed to stay silent and out of the way until now, but Díaz-Nuñez's eyes were bulging and his face was turning red. It was doubtful he could have answered Michael if he'd wanted to. She put her hand on Michael's tensed arm.

"Michael. It's possible he might be ready to talk," she said quietly. "First, though, he has to be able to breathe."

Michael drew in a deep breath and slowly eased his grip. "Well? Is she right? Do you have something to say?"

The newscaster gasped. When he could finally speak, he choked out, "The source was anonymous."

Michael's grip tightened again. "I don't believe you. I don't believe there was a source."

Díaz-Nuñez wrenched himself free and rubbed his throat. "All right, I will tell you." His expression turned smug. "My source was Paredes himself. He is the one who told me that Miguel García betrayed the organization and his people by leaking confidential information to Castro."

• • •

Back in the car, his expression grim, Michael pulled an address book from his pocket and handed it to Molly. "While I drive, you call Felipe and Ken. Tell them we're on our way to headquarters. Tell them I want as many men as possible making contact with sources to locate Paredes. If necessary we'll pull in every known member of his organization.''

"Can you do that?" Molly asked even as she took the address book and picked up his cellular phone to begin calling.

"My uncle has been missing for forty-eight hours. Based on the broadcast by Díaz-Nuñez, I think we have probable cause to suspect foul play. I'm certain I can make my boss see this my way, if the need arises."

"If the need arises," Molly repeated. "Meaning if Lucas Petty catches you pulling these people in unofficially."

He refused to meet her gaze. "Just make the calls, *por favor.*"

Though he was scheduled for an afternoon shift, Molly found Felipe already at the station.

"I'll be here when you arrive," he promised. "I heard the newscast and anticipated something like this. How is Michael's mood?"

Molly glanced at the man behind the wheel, whose expression was dark and forbidding. "About what you'd expect."

"That bad, huh? Tell him I said we'll solve this. I came in early to speak with a few of those who follow the activities of organizations such as Paredes's. You have tried to reach Ken?"

"He's next on my list."

"You won't get him. He took the day to go on the dive he promised to make. As we speak,

222

he and Teri are probably searching the bottom of Biscayne Bay. I'll call a few others and ask them to come in early to assist with the calls."

"Thanks. We'll see you soon." When she'd hung up, Molly turned to Michael. "Felipe's already checking."

"And Ken?"

"He's on that dive."

"My guess is that it'll be a waste of his time."

"He's trying to help."

"I know that, *amiga,*" he said with exaggerated patience.

Molly bit back an exasperated retort. Obviously anyone's patience would be worn thin after the tension and sleeplessness of the past couple of days. Michael, for all of his other attributes, was no saint. Rather than fuel his irritability, she dialed another number.

"Who are you calling now?"

"Walt Hazelton. Perhaps he's learned something about Paredes's whereabouts."

"I don't like relying on this correspondent for information," he said stubbornly.

"You have your sources. I have mine," Molly said evenly. Unfortunately, hers didn't know a damned thing.

"I've checked out every single place Paredes has been known to go in the past and I don't mean by calling. I spent hours driving to these places to see personally whether he was there. I did find his wife and children, however."

223

"Where?"

"They're staying with her sister. She claims to have no idea where her husband is. She says she hasn't seen or spoken to him since they left the Westchester house. She reminds me of those Mafia wives who claim not to have a clue about their husbands' activities."

In this instance, Molly could believe it. Combined with the danger of having too many people know his whereabouts, Paredes would also have a very macho attitude toward his wife's need to know anything except what was necessary for his pleasure or the care of his children. All of which gave her an idea.

"Where does this sister live?"

Hazelton gave her the address in southwest Dade. "You going to see her?"

Molly cast a look at Michael and wondered what he'd have to say about it. "I'm going to try," she said grimly.

He glanced at her as she hung up. "Try what?"

"To convince you to make a detour and let me talk with Paredes's wife."

"You know where she is?"

Molly nodded. "Walt says she doesn't know where her husband is."

"Yet you want to see her. Why?"

"Because like Tía Pilar, she may know more than she is willing to say."

"And you think you have ways of persuading

her to talk, when her husband's life might be at risk?''

Molly found his derisive tone irritating. ''I know this will come as a shock to your ego, Detective, but I do have a way with people. My presence will be far less threatening to her than yours or even Walt's.''

''Is this one of those woman-to-woman things?''

''Careful, O'Hara, your macho heritage is showing.''

He opened his mouth to reply, then snapped it shut again. Finally he said, ''What's the address?''

They found the tiny tract house off the turnpike just north of Homestead in an area that had been hard hit by Hurricane Andrew. Evidence of the violent storm was still visible in houses that remained gutted, their roofs sheared off by the powerful winds, their walls collapsed. Molly was shocked at how much remained just as it had been in the days immediately following the hurricane. She stared at it in openmouthed amazement.

''It's been nearly two years,'' she said.

''Many of these places were owned by people barely making ends meet,'' Michael reminded her. ''Some had no insurance to rebuild. Others took the money and walked away, refusing to come back after the terror of that August night and the days of hardship that followed while they waited for relief efforts.''

"I just didn't realize that it would still be like this in some places."

"What's that address again?"

When she'd given it to him, he made a final turn into a street that was like a patchwork scene of before and after. For every two or three houses that had been rebuilt, there was another one that stood as testimony to the storm's destructiveness.

María Consuela Fernández, Paredes's sister-in-law according to Walt, lived on a cul-de-sac at the end of the block in one of the houses that was livable, though it still bore signs of damage. One large picture window in front remained boarded over. The paint was badly chipped and peeling. There was even a terrible gash in the stucco exterior where some piece of flying debris had rammed the house at high speed.

But the grass was neatly cut and flowers bloomed in a bright border along the sidewalk. A new tree, barely five feet tall and skinny, its trunk still held in place by stakes and an elaborate arrangement of wires, was a testament to faith in the future.

Extracting Michael's promise to sit tight, Molly made her way to the front door through a clutter of tricycles and abandoned toys, the same clutter they'd seen outside Paredes's house.

Trepidation combined with anticipation as she rang the bell.

From inside she heard shouts of "no, *niña*, no!" just as the door opened. Molly looked down into the face of a chubby toddler whose big brown eyes gazed back solemnly. A thin, exhausted-looking woman skidded to a halt on the tile floor behind the child and scooped her up, clutching her protectively.

"Señora Paredes?" Molly said, wondering at how much younger the woman was than she'd anticipated. Perhaps a second marriage for Paredes, she mused.

There was an instant's panic in the woman's eyes that was answer enough. She started to push the door closed, but Molly held it open by bracing a shoulder against it.

"Please. I really need to speak with you. My name is Molly DeWitt. I'm not a reporter. I don't work for the police."

The woman's suspicion didn't lessen, but she did seem to relax slightly. Since it didn't seem likely that she was going to be invited in for tea, Molly decided to press on with her plea right where she was.

"May I tell you a story?" She didn't wait for a response before going on. "An old woman of whom I am very fond is very sad. She desperately misses her husband, to whom she has been married for more than forty years. He left home to go on a fishing trip several days ago and he has not returned. No one knows anything about his disappearance. It is the not knowing that breaks her heart. If her husband is dead, it would be better for her to know that. If he is not, then she would be at peace. I know that you can sympathize, because I am sure there have been times of uncertainty in your life."

The child in Señora Paredes's arms whimpered. Distractedly she put her down and the girl ran off into the house. "Why do you tell me this?" she asked Molly.

"Because you could help."

"How? I do not even know this woman."

"But her husband and your husband were very close, both in Cuba and here. Your husband might help us to locate this old man and return him to his family."

"I do not know where my husband is," she said.

The response was emphatic, but it sounded automatic, almost rehearsed. Molly regarded her intently. "Sometimes women know more than they are supposed to know," she suggested quietly.

Señora Paredes's gaze faltered. It was only a flicker, but Molly knew she had been right. "Please," she implored. "I mean your husband no harm. I just need the answers he might have."

"I understand. I sympathize with your friend, but my husband has responsibilities elsewhere," she said, her gaze now locked with Molly's. "I cannot interfere with this."

Molly couldn't be sure, but it seemed as if the woman was willing her to interpret what she was saying, to guess the answers she sought from the enigmatic response actually given. She played the words again in her mind. *Responsibilities elsewhere* triggered a faint, nagging sensation.

Suddenly the information Walt Hazelton had given her the day before came to mind. An invasion of Cuba, whether full-scale or just a tentative raid, was being staged from Key West. And this house where Señora Paredes and her children waited was squarely between the family's house in Westchester and the Florida Keys.

"He has gone to Key West, hasn't he?" Molly said.

"No sé," the woman said as she hurriedly shut the door.

But in that instant before it closed, Molly caught the truth in her eyes.

CHAPTER
EIGHTEEN

"Key West!" Michael said incredulously, when Molly joined him in the car again. "You want to drive all the way to Key West to check out some idiotic intuition of yours that that's where Paredes is?"

"What happened to all that talk about my wisdom and intelligence?"

"Logic," he said tersely.

"Yours or mine?" she shot back. "My logic tells me that Paredes is down there with his band of commandos, controlling the entire operation."

"It's a long way to go on a wild-goose chase."

Molly wasn't about to be intimidated by his obvious lack of faith. "If you don't want to make the drive, then take me home to get my car and I'll go on my own."

Their gazes clashed. Molly refused to be the first to back down. Michael finally sighed. "You're convinced of this, aren't you?"

"Absolutely."

"Then we'll go to Key West," he said, turning back onto the turnpike heading south toward Homestead and Key Largo. "Call Felipe again and tell him where we're going. Ask him to concentrate his search down there to try and pinpoint where Paredes might be. Let's just pray that he isn't on a boat bound for Cuba."

•   •   •

Between Felipe's sources at the police department and Walt Hazelton's contacts, Molly and Michael were able to come up with a half-dozen addresses in the tiny resort town of Key West of men known to be Cuban activists, who might be harboring Paredes if he was still in Florida. Just ninety miles from Cuba, the southernmost city in the U.S. had long been a haven for Cuban immigrants fleeing oppression, first from Spain and more recently from Castro's brand of communism. The first arrivals on the boat lifts from Mariel had landed here before being processed by Immigration and released to family members.

Arriving in Key West in early afternoon, Molly and Michael went from place to place, coming up empty each time. Either all were at work, which was certainly a logical assumption, given the time of day, or these activists were gathered together at some sort of central control point for whatever commando operation they were conducting. Molly was betting on the latter scenario.

"Maybe so," Michael agreed. "But I am not driving around the city looking for such a meeting. I'm starving. Let's have lunch and think this through."

At a restaurant on Duval Street, they sat in an outside garden and considered the possibilities.

"A Cuban restaurant, the old Cuban cigar factory, the San Carlos Theater," Molly suggested. "The San Carlos would be the symbolic place, since that's where Cuban independence from Spain was declared almost a hundred years ago."

Michael appeared to weigh the alternatives, then shook his head. "Too obvious and too public."

"Something at the marina?"

"Why there?"

"To be close to the boats being launched as part of the raid," she speculated.

Michael nodded thoughtfully. "Possible, but I would think Paredes would want to maintain some distance from the boats. He would want it to appear that they're leaving as usual for a fishing trip or a pleasure cruise. I doubt he'd want any hint that an armed flotilla is taking off in violation of U.S. law or that he's involved with it."

"Call the local police and see if there are places and people they keep an eye on for illegal immigration activities."

"Good idea," he said. He stopped a waiter, · found out where the pay phone was, and went inside.

While he was gone, Molly studied the clientele of the restaurant. Most were Anglos, a mix of locals on a lunch break from work, and tourists with cameras and street maps. The help, however, appeared to be largely Hispanic. Since the typical Cuban residents of Key West weren't eating lunch here, she wondered where they did tend to congregate. It was true that Paredes and his associates might not do their plotting in public, but surely they had to eat out occasionally.

The next time their waitress came by, Molly asked her about it. "Is there someplace in particular you go with your friends for Cuban food?"

The young woman named several restaurants, describing each of them. All sounded as if they were the kinds of casual places frequented by young couples and families. Molly grinned at her. "And your parents? Where would they go?"

"*Casa* Rolando," she said at once. "For special celebrations. For a simple evening with friends, however, they would go to the same places I mentioned."

"Can you tell me where they are?"

By the time Michael got back to the table, Molly had a new list of addresses. He had a similar list. Naturally the lists weren't compatible, which meant making a decision about which leads to pursue.

"Where to first?" she asked, when she'd explained her theory. "I'd like to at least try one of the restaurants. I can tell the owner I'm writing a travel article on Key West restaurants frequented by well-known people and ask who has dined there."

"And you'll just casually work Paredes's name into the conversation?" Michael said with blatant skepticism.

"Why not?"

"Because it is not . . ."

"If you accuse me of being illogical again, I'll dump the entire bottle of ketchup over your head."

He shrugged. "Okay, then. Let's just say it is not exactly an orthodox investigating technique."

"So what?"

"Indeed. So what? Okay, *amiga,* I'm a desperate man. We'll try it."

Molly discarded the upscale *Casa* Rolando in favor of the more casual spots on the theory that Paredes might figure he'd be less conspicuous there. Three restaurants later they had come up with nothing, unless her own case of caffeine jitters counted. *Café Cubano* vendors could probably make a fortune on university campuses around final exam time.

"One more," she bargained when Michael wanted to start checking out his own list of suspected hangouts.

"One more," he agreed resignedly.

The one they chose was only a block from the water and a major marina. Though it was late in the afternoon, the restaurant was still jammed, the air inside thick with a haze of cigar smoke despite health warnings and ordinances to protect against the hazards of secondary smoke.

Though he had dutifully waited in the car on the earlier tries, this time Michael insisted on coming along. "You can say I'm your photographer."

"Where's your camera?"

"I'm just on a preliminary scouting expedition with you. I'll return later for a formal photo shoot."

"Sounds like a pretty complicated ruse."

"And yours isn't?"

Molly rolled her eyes. "You have a point."

Unfortunately, after all their planning, the owner was not on the premises. The hostess, however, was a chatty young woman in her mid-twenties who clearly appreciated Michael's finer qualities. Molly wondered how he felt about being examined as a sex object. Then she decided he was probably used to it. At any rate, the hostess agreed to join them as soon as the crowd thinned out.

A waiter brought them both coffee. This time Molly insisted on decaf, which drew startled looks from the waiter and Michael. Twenty minutes later the hostess returned. She tugged a chair closer to Michael's before collapsing wearily onto it. She mostly collapsed in his direction. Another inch or two and he'd have to prop her up.

Before Molly could open her mouth to ask a single question, Michael jumped in with the announcement that he was the one doing the freelance travel piece. Molly gaped at the theft of her planned scenario. She had to admit, though, that the hostess—Lara Veciana-Peña—probably wouldn't have taken her eyes off Michael long enough to answer any question Molly asked. By contrast, she'd probably tell the sexy detective secrets she'd kept hidden from the rest of the world for her entire life. She ran red-tipped fingers through luxuriant shoulder-length black hair in a provocative gesture as she listened intently to every word that tripped from his tongue.

"Celia Cruz was in here once. Is that the sort of thing you mean?" she asked in a voice that was totally unaccented. Molly guessed she'd been born and educated right here in Key West, perhaps of immigrant parents, but more influenced by her American friends.

"Exactly," Michael said, beaming as if she'd

just given the correct answer to the trickiest question in final *Jeopardy*.

If this kept up, Molly thought she might be sick.

Lara offered up a few more celebrities in an effort to earn more of Michael's praise.

"What about writers? Politicians?" Molly asked, hoping to inch closer to the purpose of this interrogation.

Lara blinked and gazed at Molly as if she'd just noticed her presence. "Sure. Jeb Bush, you know, the ex-President's son? He came in one night with some Cuban friends. And lots of writers live right here in Key West. They're in all the time, mostly during the season, though not this time of year. Hemingway used to live here in Key West, but of course he's dead now." She named several others who were still living. Michael dutifully wrote them down.

"I was told that a Cuban looking for truly authentic food from his homeland would come here," Michael said. "In fact, the person who gave me the name of this restaurant said his friends from Miami often drive all the way down just to have a meal here."

"Yeah, I guess," Lara said vaguely. "I don't know if they're famous or anything. I've never heard of 'em, anyway."

"Are there people like this, though, on a list, so that when they call you always hold a reservation for them?"

"Sure, we have a priority customer list. My boss is real sensitive to that sort of thing."

"Could I see it?" Michael asked. "I think that's exactly the sort of thing I need for the article."

For the first time, Lara looked uneasy. "I'm not so sure he'd want it published."

Michael put his hand reassuringly over hers. Or maybe he just figured he'd give her a thrill, Molly thought in disgust as she saw the girl's eyes turn bright with something that she doubted was intelligence. She recognized lust when she saw it. She was guilty of it enough herself in Michael's presence.

"I promise not to print it as is or to reveal how I got the information," he said, gazing deeply into her eyes. "Just let me have a peek at it."

Apparently the girl read the promise of greater intimacy in Michael's expression or in his touch, because she practically ran to the reservation book.

"That was disgusting," Molly said under her breath.

He grinned at her unrepentantly. "Worked, didn't it?"

"Just don't be surprised when she turns up in Miami looking for love."

He scowled at her as Lara rejoined them and spread a typed list on the table. Molly tried to get a look at it, but it was upside down and she didn't think standing up to peer anxiously over Michael's shoulder was the thing to do. And Michael, damn him, didn't reveal a damn thing in his expression.

He jotted down a couple of notes. "Any of these people in this week?"

Lara shook her head. "But I took a reservation earlier for tonight from Señor Hernández. He said he was bringing some very important people from out of town."

Molly recognized the name at once. It had been on the contact list given to them by both Felipe and Walt Hazelton. "Did he mention who these friends were?"

"Not to me," she said.

Molly's spirits sank.

"But," Lara said, "my boss said we should pay special attention because this man he's bringing could one day be president of a free Cuba."

Molly shot a triumphant look at Michael. If that wasn't Orestes León Paredes, then she didn't know who it could be.

CHAPTER
NINETEEN

Michael used his considerable persuasive skills to convince the cooperative, smitten Lara to give him and Molly a dinner reservation at a table across the restaurant, but with a clear view of the one being held for Señor Hernández and his party.

"You will not disturb them," she asked worriedly.

It was the first indication that she didn't entirely trust the newfound love of her life. Trust was always the first thing to go, Molly noted dryly.

"Absolutely not," Michael promised, his expression all innocence and reassurance.

Molly was astounded at how easily he blatantly lied to the poor woman. It raised some interesting questions about the things he'd whispered in her ear the past few nights. Of course, given her own willingness to bend veracity for the sake of getting a piece of relevant information, maybe she didn't have a lot of room to talk.

When they left the restaurant, Molly insisted on finding a hotel room, taking a shower, and buying a new dress for dinner, not necessarily in that order.

"Why don't I drop you off back on Duval Street to shop?" Michael suggested. "I'll get the hotel room, pick you up in a couple of hours, and we can take that shower together."

"Are you sure you'd prefer sharing a shower with me, rather than your new conquest?" she inquired crankily.

"That was only business, *querida*."

Molly was beginning to notice he pulled out the more affectionate term when he wanted something. "Just how far were you willing to take this *business* in order to get answers?"

"I suppose you have never flirted with a man to get what you wanted?"

"Never," Molly said piously.

"Liar," he accused. "I myself have been the victim of your wiles."

She turned on him indignantly. "Michael O'Hara, I never flirted with you to get information."

He grinned unrepentantly. "Ah, then it was only because you wished to flirt with me? Perhaps you've been hoping all this time to seduce me?''

Molly glared at him as the car stopped for a group of pedestrians crossing the street. She opened the door, got out, then slammed it shut. She walked around to Michael's side and leaned in the window. "Better make that two rooms, *amigo*.''

● ● ●

It was amazing how little petty annoyances vanished in a puff of steam, during a long, friendly shower, Molly thought as she and Michael were led to their table that night by someone other than Lara. With the hostess absent, Molly found she could hardly recall what her argument with Michael had been about.

They had arrived fifteen minutes earlier than their quarry, so they would already be seated when the others turned up. With any luck, Paredes wouldn't even notice them until they'd managed to eavesdrop on quite a bit of the conversation.

Actually eavesdrop was a polite description for it. Michael had managed to plant a tiny transmitter in a wall plug near the other table and had put a pocket-size receiver in Molly's handbag.

"Isn't this illegal?" Molly inquired when he returned from his surreptitious trip to install the fake plug in the wall outlet. "I mean, don't you need a court order or something before you go tapping somebody's dinner conversation?''

"I would if I had any intention of taking this to court. I'm just an innocent citizen trying to locate a missing relative. The ethics are questionable, but right now the only thing I give a damn about is Miguel's safety.''

"But what if you hear them plotting something illegal. You won't even be able to turn them in, will you?''

"An anonymous tip," he said with a shrug. "It would then be up to the authorities to follow up in a by-the-book manner." He slanted a curious look at her. "Why so worried about my ethics?''

"Because you seem to be breaking every rule you live by. I'm just wondering how you're going to feel about that when this is over.''

"If I learn the truth about Miguel, the price will not be too high.''

Molly wondered about that, but she couldn't debate the point with him because a handful of men in the Hernández party arrived and were led to the table across the room. Based on the deference being paid him, Molly picked out the tall, well-dressed man with silver hair as Señor Hernández. He, like all the others, looked like a successful middle-class businessman. Despite the season and the summer heat, they wore dark business suits, expensive dress shirts with monogrammed cuffs, and silk ties. She suspected all of them had been told to tuck their checkbooks in their pockets for the occasion. Or perhaps they were the types who'd just peel off hundred-dollar bills from a bundle held together by a sterling-silver money clip. Half a dozen cellular phones were placed on the table, yet another indication of their success.

When Orestes Léon Paredes walked in, escorted by two men the size of small tanks, Molly regarded him with astonishment. The military fatigues had been replaced by a suit that transformed him into a handsome, powerful-looking figure. Though he was shorter than many of the other men, his commanding presence immediately overshadowed them. Perhaps it had something to do with that charisma Michael had mentioned. The only person who was his equal in presence was Señor Hernández, who was treating all of his guests with the manner of a benevolent dictator.

Molly tried to listen to the snatches of conversation being picked up by the transmitter. Michael reached over and touched her shoulder gently.

"Do not stare so intently at your purse," he advised mildly. "People may wonder if it is speaking to you."

She shot upright. "Sorry. Can you hear them?"

"Enough."

"What are they talking about?"

"The Florida Marlins' latest victory over the Atlanta Braves, I believe."

"Oh," she said flatly.

"Never fear. They will get to the point of this gathering soon."

Molly prayed he was right. Michael's tone was calm, but there was no mistaking the tension in the set of his jaw and the watchfulness in his eyes. She wondered how long he would wait patiently before physically trying to force Paredes to give him the answers he sought about Miguel.

Forced to make a show of being there for dinner, they ordered a meal of paella, mainly because Michael knew it would take longer to prepare and guarantee them a reason for lingering. When it eventually came, it might as well have been sawdust for all the attention they paid it. Their worried waiter asked repeatedly if there was some problem with their meal. Michael waved him away, assuring him that their appetites were simply overwhelmed by the delicious seafood dish.

"Damn," Michael muttered irritably when the waiter had been temporarily placated.

"What?"

"I'm beginning to wonder if they are ever going to get beyond these pleasantries after all."

"What if it turns out to be just a friendly get-together?"

Michael shook his head. "At the least, I expect Paredes to ask for money from these men to support his efforts. These are not men who would take up arms and raid Cuba themselves, but they would be sympathetic.'' His expression turned cynical. ''After all, in a free Cuba their businesses would stand to make a small fortune, especially with such well-established influence with a new government headed by their close friend, Orestes León Paredes.''

Eventually cigars were passed around, and a haze of smoke rose from the table. Michael nodded in satisfaction. ''Good. They will get to the bottom line now.''

Listening intently, Molly picked out a smattering of familiar words, most of them bitterly spoken, unflattering descriptions of Fidel Castro, along with talk of his failing health and the already-failed economy.

Paredes spoke with feeling. As near as Molly could translate it, he said adamantly, ''The end is near for Fidel. I will see to it.''

Cheers and a toast greeted his statement, along with promises of support. If she hadn't known the context, Molly would have thought it the same as any other political gathering to generate early support for a candidate. She'd been to a few dinners for prospective candidates for local offices that had been no less hard-sell pitches for money.

''Have they said anything at all about the raids?'' she asked Michael.

''Nothing. It appears that is something they

dare not speak of in public, or else they talk in terms so vague that no one else can accuse them of plotting the overthrow of a foreign government."

Interestingly enough, it also appeared that no money was going to change hands. Perhaps one of Paredes's minions would take up a collection after the leader had discreetly departed. Even now, he was standing up to go, a royal taking leave of his subjects with a slight bow and no looking back.

"What . . ." Molly began before she realized that Michael was already on his feet, clearly intending to intersect Paredes's path at the door.

Before she could make a move to follow, she noticed another man slipping through the shadows on the far side of the restaurant. Just as she recognized Herman Gómez-Ortega, she saw that he had something in his hand, though he held it discreetly at his side.

A gun, she realized with a dawning sense of disbelief. In her haste to warn Michael, she knocked over her chair and bumped into several people as she ran toward the door, trailed by a waiter assuming he was about to be stiffed for the check.

In the back of her mind, Molly couldn't help seeing Paredes's house as it had looked after an assault rifle had blown out the front windows. Was he here tonight in his organization role to protect Paredes or did he intend to repeat the assassination attempt that had failed in Miami? Either way, Michael was in danger, she thought as she ran blindly outside after them.

She was afraid to shout a warning, because she wasn't entirely sure who was armed and who was on which side. Before she could figure out how to get past Gómez-Ortega, she saw Paredes grab Michael's arm, spin him around, and yank him behind the cover of a van parked down the block.

Suddenly men appeared from every direction, all armed and all wearing flak jackets with various official designations on the backs. Apparently the neon letters were meant to help distinguish the good guys from the bad. Molly hated to be the one to tell them, but it didn't help. Everyone on the goddamned street looked downright dangerous. A man whose flak jacket identified him in neon orange letters as POLICE strong-armed Molly back inside the restaurant doorway.

"Stay put," he said, and left her there, trembling violently and face-to-face with their stunned waiter, who'd just caught on that this was no ordinary turn of events involving a couple of deadbeats. As rattled as she was, Molly managed to snatch a handful of bills from her purse and shove them into his hand.

Not thirty seconds later there was a hail of gunfire, accompanied by shouts and screams. Then dead silence. Molly couldn't have stayed where she was if her own life had depended on it. She kept visualizing Michael in the grasp of Orestes León Paredes, a man not known for his peaceful intent.

She shrugged off the detaining hand of the waiter and edged out the doorway and peered down the block. Police officials were kneeling on the pavement over what appeared to be a body.

Smothering a scream with her hand, Molly crept toward the macabre scene, which was bathed in the glow of a streetlamp. Not until she was almost on top of the police and before she could identify the fallen victim did she see a movement from the direction of the van where she'd last seen Michael.

First a policeman emerged, followed by Paredes himself. He didn't look to be in custody. Finally, when her breath seemed to have stopped all together, she saw Michael, his gaze searching the scene as frantically as her own. By the time he spotted her, she was already running.

He held out his arms, then enfolded her in an embrace. "You are okay, *amiga?*"

She swallowed a sob. "Now that you're here, yes," she said, her voice steady. She looked up into Michael's ashen face. "They shot Herman, didn't they?"

"Yes."

"Because of his attack on Paredes's house the other day?"

"That and his plan to kill him tonight."

"But why would he want to kill Paredes? I still don't understand."

"Neither do I. Perhaps when things have settled down a bit, Paredes will explain it to us."

At that precise moment, the exile commander walked over to them. Michael held out his hand. "I owe you my life, señor."

"De nada." His grin turned rueful. "Had I not dragged you to safety, you would have persisted in questioning me in plain view of Herman and we both would have been shot to death. I was not prepared to die, not at the hands of a traitor."

"You call Herman Gómez-Ortega a traitor," Molly said with evident confusion. "I thought he was your chief military advisor."

"For a time that is how I thought of him, as well," he said with obvious pain. "It was only recently, in the last few days, in fact, that I learned the truth."

"What truth?"

"He was sent here as a spy by Castro. That is how he won his release from prison, by agreeing to infiltrate our organization and feed information to Cuban Intelligence. When I was told by American agents of their suspicions, I called them liars. But with so much at stake, I could not afford to ignore the possibilities. With the assistance of my most loyal associates, we devised a means of learning the truth."

He grasped Michael's shoulders. "Your uncle, Miguel García, was vital to our plan. It was his heroic offer to act as the bait which enabled us to trap Herman into showing his hand.''

Michael went absolutely still. ''You used my uncle as bait?'' he said in a voice as cold as ice. ''How? Just today Díaz-Nuñez said you had called my uncle a traitor.''

Paredes waved off the remark. ''He misunderstood. I told him we had discovered a traitor and that we were dealing with him. Because of Miguel García's disappearance, he leapt to a wrong conclusion. It was not unexpected. Even with such errors in judgment, I find him useful.''

''Useful?'' Michael repeated. ''Is that all any of these men are to you, just pawns in your games? Explain how my uncle was useful.''

''We made it known he was to be the point man in our raid.'' Paredes said quietly. His burning gaze never left Michael's. ''And, as we anticipated, when he took his boat out on Sunday, the Cuban authorities were waiting to take him captive.''

Molly gasped softly.

Michael's expression turned absolutely deadly. ''You sent my uncle to sea knowing that he would wind up in a Cuban jail?'' He jerked away from the other man's grasp. ''Look over your shoulder, Paredes. One day I will see that you share the same fate as Miguel García,'' he vowed.

CHAPTER
TWENTY

"How will I tell Tía Pilar?" Michael asked over and over as they drove back to Miami. "How can I tell her that Miguel is back in his beloved Havana, but that he is being held in some harsh Cuban prison where he will probably die?"

The question was rhetorical. He never looked to Molly for an answer. He just spoke and then fell into a brooding silence. It was just as well because she had no answers. She was as horrified as he was that sweet, gentle Tío Miguel was imprisoned in Cuba by a government that would treat him as a traitor. It was possible he would be shot, as others had been, to set an example for those thinking of staging future commando raids. A tear slid down her cheek as she considered that possibility.

It was after midnight when they reached

Miami, but Michael drove straight to Little Havana. Rather than going to see Pilar, however, he went to Pedro's restaurant.

They found his uncle nursing a cup of *café Cubano,* surrounded by a group of men actively debating the candidacies of two people running for the Dade County Commission. One was a high-profile attorney, originally from Havana, with ties to the powerful Latin Builders Association. The other was a woman, head of her own interior design company, active in the arts. What seemed to be splitting the group about evenly was the fact that the man had once attended a professional seminar in Latin America at which Fidel had been a speaker. For some, that alone was enough to disqualify him from holding a public office representing the Cuban exile community.

Pedro glanced up and caught sight of them. He motioned them over, but Michael shook his head. *"Por favor,"* he said, and indicated a table in an empty section that had already been closed for the night.

Instantly, Pedro's expression sobered. "You have news, is that it?" he said as he joined them. "And from the look on your faces, it is not good."

"No, it's not good," Michael agreed.

"Miguel is dead?"

"Some would say that would be better news," Michael said, urging his uncle to sit.

Pedro clung to Michael's arms, his gaze fixed on Michael's face. "My God, do not tell me he has been taken captive? Is that what you are saying?"

"I'm sorry," Michael whispered, his voice catching as Pedro slowly sank down onto a chair, his complexion gray. Michael's worried gaze sought his uncle's. "Are you okay?"

"I will be fine."

"Fine?" Michael said angrily. "How can that be? How can any of us be fine again?" He slammed his fist on the table. "Damn them all to hell!"

"Tell me," Pedro insisted quietly.

Michael repeated everything that they had learned from Paredes in Key West. When he'd recited the whole complicated story, Pedro made him go through it all once more, as if he couldn't believe what he was hearing.

"I will begin making calls in the morning," Michael promised, his anger now under control. In a way the calm was worse. His voice was cold and emotionless. "I will call our senators and our representatives. I'll call the State Department. Perhaps it is not too late to bring him back home. What use has Castro for one old man?"

Pedro clasped Michael's hands in his own. "I know you will do what you can. Remember something, though. This was Miguel's choice. No matter how badly it has turned out, you cannot lay the blame entirely with Paredes. Allow Miguel the dignity of respecting his decision."

The simple request seemed to take Michael by surprise. Slowly and with obvious effort, he let the last traces of his anger die. Finally, he nodded. "I will do my best," he said wearily. "But something tells me that knowing Miguel did what he felt he had to do will be cold comfort to Tía Pilar."

"Perhaps not," Tío Pedro agreed. "That is why all of us must be strong for her. We are a family, Michael. We stand together, and from that we will draw whatever strength it takes to get through the coming days."

• • •

Despite the lateness of the hour, the García house was crowded with family—Pilar, Elena, Rosa, Michael's cousins. Molly wasn't sure she belonged among them on such a tragic occasion, but Michael's grip on her hand convinced her that he needed her there, whatever the others thought of her intrusion.

Surprisingly, though, the mood was oddly euphoric when they arrived. Apparently several bottles of wine had been consumed with a meal sent over from the restaurant by Pedro. Rosa was even singing along with an old Cuban ballad to the applause of her nieces and nephews.

Standing in the doorway observing the light-hearted moment, Michael and Pedro exchanged looks. Molly wondered which of them would spoil it by revealing the news of Miguel's fate. Apparently that time was to be put off. Glasses of wine were pressed into their hands by Elena.

"Sit. Rosa has been singing all of the old songs for us."

"She has not sung in a long time," Pedro noted.

"*Sí,*" Elena agreed quietly. "But it seems to keep Pilar's spirits high. Look, have you seen her looking so happy since all of this began? She has been that way since dinnertime."

"Perhaps it is the wine," Pedro suggested.

"More likely the call she had from an old friend. They talked for some time. It seemed to give her comfort."

"Whatever it was, I'm glad for her," Michael said, giving his uncle a pointed look. Pedro nodded. Molly guessed they intended to postpone telling Pilar anything, at least for the moment.

Molly, however, was puzzled by Tía Pilar's sudden shift in mood. Compared to earlier visits, this time her expression was actually serene. The older woman looked as if she'd found some sort of inner peace, as if she already knew about her husband's fate and had accepted it. It was not what Molly had expected after watching her state of mind deteriorate hour by hour in the early aftermath of Miguel's disappearance.

Trying to make sense of it, Molly crossed the room and took a seat beside Tía Pilar.

"You are feeling better, then?" she said.

"I must be strong," Pilar said with a faraway smile, her gaze on Rosa as the lyrics of yet another song filled the tiny room. "For Miguel."

"I understand you had a phone call earlier this evening, just before dinner. It was from an old friend?" Molly said, wondering if it was remotely possible that what she was beginning to think could be true.

Pilar regarded her sharply. "Who told you this?"

"Elena. She said the call seemed to lift your spirits."

"It was nothing," Pilar said.

"Elena said you spoke for quite some time."

Pilar's expression suddenly and conveniently went blank. *"No comprendo."*

Molly watched her closely. "I think you do understand, Pilar. It was Miguel, wasn't it? Did he call you from Cuba?"

"You don't know what you are saying," she said, suddenly agitated. "We don't know where Miguel is."

"No, *we* don't," Molly agreed. "Not exactly, anyway. But I think you do. He's safe, isn't he?"

Pilar glanced around worriedly. "Please, you must not say this."

"But the others deserve to know, especially Michael. He has been worried sick. Tonight he learned from a source that his uncle might be in a Havana prison, but that's not true, is it?"

"I cannot say anything. Miguel made me promise. The danger is too great."

Molly took her hand. "No, Tía Pilar, the danger is over," she told her gently. "You can tell the truth now."

Michael joined them just then. He looked from his aunt's distressed face to Molly and back again. "What is it? What truth are you keeping from us, Tía?"

"Tell him," Molly insisted.

Pilar's hands trembled. She linked them together in her lap to keep them still.

"Tía, what's going on?"

"It is Miguel," she said at last. "I spoke to him earlier tonight." She lifted her gaze to Michael. "He is alive. He is safe."

CHAPTER
TWENTY-ONE

Before any of them could fully absorb what Tía Pilar was telling them, the front door opened and Miguel García walked in. Dressed as always in khaki pants and a freshly starched *guayabera,* he had the unmistakable look of a man who had just completed a successful mission. His eyes, filled with happiness and affection, were pinned on his wife. For this moment, at least, the sadness had been banished and the strength and purpose of a young man were reflected there.

While Pilar waited patiently, he was immediately surrounded by his emotional children. Tears were shed openly. Molly's own tears were silent, but no less heartfelt.

She looked for Michael and found him standing alone on the perimeter of the scene, his eyes suspiciously damp, his expression filled with longing. In that brief instant, Molly thought she caught a glimpse of the young boy who'd never had a father, who had never quite dared to admit how deeply he loved this uncle for fear that he could lose him as easily as he once had his mother. In the past few days that loss had been vividly transformed from nightmare to reality.

Molly moved to Michael's side and slipped her hand in his as Tío Miguel embraced his weeping wife and attempted to soothe her and make her laugh, even as she scolded him for frightening them all so badly.

"How could he have put us all through so much heartache?" Michael said to Molly. He sounded as if the betrayal by someone he loved so dearly had cut right through him.

"Ask him," she urged.

"I don't need to ask. It's the cause," he said bitterly. "It is always the cause."

"Ask him," she repeated.

At first she didn't think he would take her advice. Then, with a sigh, he took a reluctant step toward the uncle he so clearly loved. Catching the belligerent set to his jaw, she called him back. "Michael!"

He turned.

"Don't just ask. Listen to what he has to say."

He gave her a faint grin. "Yes, *querida*, I will listen."

In the end, they all listened as Miguel spun

his tale of intrigue and international spies. To Molly it was something out of a political thriller, a world that until now had never touched her own. She still wasn't sure she entirely understood such passion and loyalty for a country left behind so long ago. Perhaps without the experience of exile, she could never fully understand the actions of men like Miguel García and Orestes León-Paredes.

"We had to know," Miguel explained to Michael in Spanish. Pedro sat by Molly's side and translated for her benefit.

"If any of us were ever to trust each other again, we had to know if what the Americans said of Gómez-Ortega was true. He and he alone was told by Paredes that I would be launching the first stage of an assault on Sunday. I took my boat to just inside Cuban waters. Any closer to shore and we knew the soldiers would capture it at once and we would never know for certain if they had been tipped by a traitor inside our organization. It was necessary for them to seek out a boat they had been anticipating."

"How did you escape, Papá?" one of his sons asked.

"I dropped anchor, then launched my raft and motored to a pickup point a mile outside Cuban territorial waters. There another boat picked me up and carried me to safety in Key West. For the past few days I have been in hiding there to keep Gómez-Ortega from learning the truth. It was necessary to see how far he would go."

He gazed up at Michael, then reached out and clutched his hand. "I am deeply sorry for what happened to you, my son. You were not meant to find the boat, the soldiers were. And when they did, it was meant to blow them up. Instead, you were the one nearly killed. Had anything happened to you, my boy, I could never have forgiven myself."

"Are you so sure you would not have called it a noble sacrifice?" Michael demanded angrily.

"I would have called it a tragedy and the greatest loss of my life," Miguel replied softly.

Michael drew in a deep breath, but trusting in his uncle's love did not come so easily. "Why didn't you call? Why didn't you let us know you were alive? After the plan had been set in motion, couldn't you have let us know you were safe?"

"It was necessary to keep the charade alive, to let Gómez-Ortega think that the attack was soon to be launched. We hoped he would become desperate, as he did. When he tried to kill Paredes in his own home, we knew for certain, then, that it was true. He was a spy for Castro. He was willing to kill for him. We staged the scene in Key West for the benefit of Gómez-Ortega, after alerting American Intelligence agents of what we knew." He closed his eyes and sighed, then looked at Michael. "And again, you were nearly caught in the crossfire."

"Another trap," Michael said wearily. "When will it end?"

"When Cuba is free," Miguel said softly, but emphatically. "Only then."

At Miguel's words, Pedro lifted his glass of wine. *"A una Cuba libre!"*

"A una Cuba libre!" the others echoed.

Michael was the last to lift his glass and repeat the phrase. When he did, his gaze met his uncle's, and a tender, patient smile touched Miguel's lips. It was a moment of shared acceptance and of a deep and abiding love, if not of understanding.

Miguel stood slowly then and held his glass high, his expression a mixture of pride and fierce determination. "Next time in Havana!"

September, 1994

Dear Readers:

One of the joys—and challenges—of living in Miami is its multiethnic nature. After living in Miami for a few years, I took Spanish at Miami-Dade Community College. Other than speaking with a French accent leftover from college, I thought I was beginning to grasp the vocabulary at least, rather well. I quickly learned, however, that admitting to speaking Spanish even a little—*un poco*—was a mistake. Inevitably those to whom I made this admission chattered at a pace that left me reeling. I adapted much more quickly to Cuban food, which I love.

The sorrow and anger of Cuban exile, though, were much more difficult to comprehend. As a newspaper columnist who wrote about television and radio, I was quickly plunged into this world when Cuban radio commentator Emilio Milian's car was bombed, very nearly killing him. Other bombings followed during the seventies, protests of a business's dealings with Cuba or of a gallery's showing of works by artists still living in Cuba. The controversy over Castro's stranglehold on Cuba continues to be hotly debated today, but it has become more a matter of passionate beliefs, than violent acts.

I hope through Molly and Michael, you are able to experience just some of the emotions felt by Miami's Cuban exiles and their Anglo neighbors. As always, I would love to hear from you. You may write me at P.O. Box 490326, Key Biscayne, FL 33149. A self-addressed, stamped envelope is appreciated for a reply.

My best, as always,

Sherryl Woods

Be sure to catch Sherryl Wood's
next exciting mystery,

HOT TICKET

Coming soon from Dell.

CHAPTER
ONE

Given his penchant for excess, it was somehow fitting that Richard Winthrop Newton, better known as King, keeled over dead in a plate of oysters Rockefeller, while watching his thoroughbred stallion falter at the finish line at South Florida's historic Hialeah Park. The odds-on favorite had come in second in the Kentucky Derby prep race, the Flamingo Stakes. It had been a stunning defeat for both horse and owner.

Molly DeWitt, who'd been procrastinating like crazy down in the lushly landscaped paddock area, arrived upstairs in the Turf Club with its unimpeded view of the finish line, just in time to see her father's best friend and top legal client being placed on a stretcher. The blanket over his face and the sobs of hysteria from his wife, Mary Elizabeth Tyler Newton, and Molly's mother pretty much told the story.

1

The King was dead. Long live the King.

Molly felt Michael O'Hara's grasp on her elbow tighten. His dark brown eyes studied her intently. "What is it, *amiga?*"

"The man they're taking away . . ." she began, her voice catching. She attributed the faltering to shock, not any great love for the man who'd died. She'd never been wild about him or his social-climbing wife, though this was hardly the time to announce that to the world. Months of Thursday afternoon deportment lessons had drilled that into her.

"You know him," he said gently, misinterpreting her silence for dismay. "I'm sorry. He is the man who was here with your parents?"

Molly nodded. One of the best things about being involved with a homicide detective, she'd discovered over the last few months, was that very little surprised him. He also could add two and two to get four faster than the average calculator. Her handsome companion was closely studying the little throng of people around the table where King Newton had apparently died—two women, a handful of men. Everyone else in the vicinity was pointedly ignoring the scene, possibly because the tenth race was being run, possibly because they, too, had been drilled in etiquette from birth.

"The people who were there with him?" he asked, his eyes alert for any little detail.

When they had first met, Molly had attributed this delightful masculine attentiveness to her charisma. Then she'd discovered it was nothing more

2

than an occupational skill. Michael looked over everything and everyone as if it were a crime scene and they were suspects. For all she knew at this point, it was and they were.

At the moment, if if would keep her from joining the gathering of mourners, she'd describe every person in the room she recognized. "First, there's his wife, Mary Elizabeth Tyler Newton, of the Virginia Tylers," Molly began, knowing how important the latter was to Mary Elizabeth.

"The one who looks as if she dressed for a spread in *Town and Country*?"

Molly studied the two women standing side by side, their hands clutched. As far as she could tell, every female in the room looked as if they'd dressed for the classy magazine. She assessed her mother's flamingo pink raw silk suit and straw hat, compared to Mary Newton's more subtle navy and white ensemble. She glanced around at the other designer dresses and showy hats.

Since she couldn't tell for certain which woman's attire had drawn Michael's attention, she just said, "The one in navy blue, who looks as if she can't quite believe her husband is responsible for all this commotion, is Mrs. Newton. She finds scenes appalling, very low class. My mother's wearing the pink getup. She really likes to get into these theme occasions. I'm sure she was very careful to choose a color that would complement the flock of flamingos in the infield."

"And your father?"

Molly glanced around and shook her head. "I don't see him."

"Perhaps he has gone to speak with the doctors or the track officials."

"More than likely," Molly agreed. Actually, if she knew anything at all about Jonathan Richardson III, he was raising a ruckus somewhere. For that matter, he was probably in the kitchen threatening to sue whoever prepared those oysters Rockefeller. He probably hadn't even waited to discover whether the dish actually had anything to do with King's death. He won a lot of cases with the sheer force of his intimidating personality.

Molly tried to summon up a stirring of sympathy for the dead man, but she felt hypocritical. She'd never much liked King Newton or his wife. King was boisterous, crude, and politically somewhere to the right of the KKK. His wife wielded her social graces like a stiletto, carving up anyone in her path whom she considered beneath her. To Molly's very deep regret, they were a good match for her own parents.

Just this once, however, Molly supposed she ought to be grateful to King. His death certainly took the pressure off of her for this dreaded and long-postponed reunion with her parents.

She glanced up at Michael. "I suppose it's too late to take a powder."

"*Amiga,* you managed to dawdle outside through eight races. You gave an entire lecture on the historical significance of this track. We practically counted the damned flowers. We ate pizza,

4

when I'd been looking forward to a tender filet. I think it's past time to put in an appearance. If you really didn't want to see your parents, you never should have agreed to come in the first place."

Molly scowled at him. "You make it sound so simple, as if saying no to Jonathan Richardson is a piece of cake."

He grinned. "You used to say it to me very effectively. Am I less persuasive than your father?"

"It's not the same thing at all. You were after sex. My father wants to own me." She found herself smiling despite herself. "You'll notice that I didn't hold out against you forever."

"Do you regret that?"

"Never."

"Then perhaps you will not regret mending fences with your parents either."

"Perhaps," she said, but she didn't believe it. From the moment her parents had sided with her ex-husband during the divorce, there had been an ever-widening rift between them and Molly. She wasn't sure she'd ever be able to forgive them for blaming her, rather than Hal DeWitt, for the marriage's failure. Until her father's phone call last week insisting that she join them at the track today, she'd figured on remaining estranged from them for the rest of her life. The prospect had been only marginally disturbing and more for her son's sake, than her own.

Before she could dwell on that and get her anger all stirred up one more time, her mother caught sight of her.

"Oh, darling, there you are," Genevieve Henley Richardson cried, rushing to embrace Molly as if they'd parted on friendly terms only days before. "It's all so terrible. King collapsed, right at the end of the race. Mary and I were looking through the binoculars. Neither of us could absorb that disastrous outcome. I mean how is it possible that a million-dollar horse with impeccable bloodlines could be beaten by some filly whose sire nobody had ever heard of? The only race that horse had ever won was in Arkansas, for goodness sake. Anyway, that was when we heard the crash. There was King, on the table." She shuddered. "I still can't believe he's dead."

Before Molly could offer a word of comfort, Genevieve Henley Richardson's expression changed from dismay to that critical look Molly knew all too well. She braced herself.

"Where have you been, darling?" her mother asked, her tone peevish. "We expected you hours ago for lunch. I didn't know what to say to Mary and King about your appalling manners."

"I told father I might not be able to get here before the ninth race. Michael was working." Which he had been . . . until about 11 A.M.

At the mention of the man standing quietly beside Molly, her mother looked Michael O'Hara over from head to toe and then, despite his gorgeous body and spiffy designer suit, she visibly dismissed him. After all, he wasn't Hal DeWitt, Molly thought, reading her mother's mind. Worse, no doubt, he was obviously of Hispanic descent, despite his very Irish name.

"Yes, well, that's not important now. You're here," she said, turning back to Molly. "I'm sure you'll be able to pitch right in and help Mary get through this terrible ordeal. How does one go about making the necessary arrangements under these circumstances?"

"I could take care of that, if you like," Michael offered. As a Metro-Dade homicide detective, Michael had more than a passing acquaintance with procedures to be followed in the event of untimely deaths, no matter the prominence of the deceased or the cause of his demise.

Molly's mother barely spared him a glance. She probably figured he'd been brought along just to deal with such troublesome little details.

"Yes, that would be lovely, I'm sure," she said, clearly prepared not to give the messy matter of death another thought. "Now come, darling, Mary's over here. She's quite distraught, as you might imagine. We must get her out of here the moment your father returns."

Shooting Michael an apologetic look, Molly trailed after her mother. He winked at her. "I'll see what I can find out," he promised, heading off in the same direction as King's body.

There was a flurry of activity around Mary Newton. Her navy wide-brimmed hat with its white piping was askew. Her normally smooth, ash blond hairstyle looked as if she'd walked through a wind tunnel. Mascara tracked down her cheeks. The effect was worsened because she kept brushing impatiently at her tears. Molly was amazed the self-absorbed woman hadn't plucked her gold compact from her purse to repair the damage. Possibly she was reveling in the unexpected attention, after all.

"I'm terribly sorry, Mrs. Newton," Molly said, though she had the feeling Mary Newton had barely noticed her arrival.

"Thank you, dear," the older woman murmured, never once looking up from the lace-edged handkerchief she was twisting into a knot in her lap. "What will I do? What ever will I do without my King?"

Molly's mother knelt down beside her and began mouthing all the appropriately consoling words that Molly couldn't muster. Since she wasn't able to offer anything constructive, she strolled around the table, which was now littered not only with the congealed remains of lunch, but a variety of disgusting trash from the medical emergency team. The plate of half-eaten oysters Rockefeller remained right where it had been. Molly delicately sniffed for any hint of spoilage. The food smelled fine to her.

The table had been set for six, the two extra places obviously meant for Molly and Michael. It looked as though someone had sat in one of the empty chairs, at least long enough to leave a dirty wine glass there. In fact, it appeared everyone had been drinking wine, except King. There were several empty tumblers that had once contained scotch lined up beside his place. The last glass still had about two fingers of the liquid, along with a rapidly melting ice cube. Nothing out of the ordinary there, as near as she could tell.

Even that extra wine glass wasn't terribly odd. People table-hopped all the time at events like this, stopping by just long enough to share a drink, pass along a hot tip on the next race, commiserate over losses, then move on to other old cronies. It would be interesting to know who had left it, though, and whether that person had still been around when King keeled over.

Obviously, she'd been spending too much time around murder investigations, Molly chided herself. She was getting to be as suspicious as Michael.

Just then she heard a stir of commotion and looked up in time to see her father weaving through the crowd toward them, his expression thunderous. "I've never heard anything so ridiculous in all my life," he complained to anyone within hearing distance, which was most of the people in the Turf Club and probably those outside in the grandstand as well.

Her expression alarmed, Molly's mother immediately flew to his side. "What is it? What on earth's the matter, Jonathan?"

Before he could reply, a grim-faced Michael returned, accompanied by two uniformed police officers. Molly was beginning to get really lousy vibes.

Ignoring her father, who hadn't even noticed her yet, she kept her gaze pinned on Michael.

"I think perhaps we should all go into the manager's office," Michael suggested quietly.

Molly watched her mother's mouth set in a who-do-you-think-you-are frown. Genevieve Richardson looked toward her husband.

"He's right. There's no sense getting into this with every old gossip listening in."

"Getting into what? Jonathan, I demand that you tell us what is going on before we budge one single inch."

"That's enough, Genevieve," he commanded in a booming voice. "Mary," he said more softly. "Come along."

Mary was considerably more amenable than his wife. She rose and swept from the room with a regal air, leaving Molly's mother to trail along, her expression shifting from astonishment to fury and back again.

Molly waited until they were out of earshot before meeting Michael's gaze. "King didn't choke."

"No."

"It wasn't a heart attack?"

"No, *amiga*. The medical examiner will have to await a few test results, but he believes more than likely your parents' friend was murdered. He suspects something lethal was slipped into his drink."

Molly saw that one police officer was quietly gathering up the assorted glasses from in front of King's place, along with his plate of food. "No won-

der my father is in such a snit. He is no doubt royally
ticked off that his best frend was murdered right
under his nose and he didn't have a clue."

"Or that he is on the short list of suspects,"
Michael reminded her.

"Daddy? You must be kidding."

"He was there, seated right next to the man.
Opportunity, yes?"

"What about motive? I could see Mary killing
her husband before I could see my father doing it."

Michael patted her hand. "Do not worry *amiga*.
She's on the short list as well, along with your
mother. If we'd gotten up here a little earlier, we'd
be suspects, too."

"Now aren't you glad you settled for pizza?" she
said, taking one last look around the apparent crime
scene. "Being questioned in a murder investigation
would be really lousy for your career."

"No doubt," he agreed dryly. "Are you ready to
join the others?"

She started to follow, then spotted King's jacket
lying on the seat of one of the chairs. "Wait." Before he could tell her not to touch a piece of evidence, Molly snatched it up, automatically feeling in
the pockets for items that should be removed before
it made a final trip to the dry cleaners. She felt only
a few pieces of paper, losing tickets on the day's
earlier races, no doubt.

Taking them from the pocket, she glanced
through the half-dozen tickets. As she'd guessed,
most were for the first eight races, but there was one

for the ninth, a five hundred dollar bet on number ten, plus an equal amount on the perfecta with the ten horse on top and the six horse second.

Praying she was wrong, she turned to Michael. "Do you still have today's racing program?"

He plucked it from his pocket, his expression quizzical. "What's wrong?"

"Maybe nothing. I'll know in a minute."

She flipped through to the page listing the horses in the ninth feature race, the Flamingo Stakes. As she'd recalled, King's stallion, Always A King, had been number six. Number ten, Not A Lady, was the horse that won the race. The program odds listed it as likely to go off at forty to one. If the final odds had even come close, that winning ticket in King's pocket was worth $20,000. Molly couldn't begin to calculate the winnings he would have collected on the perfecta.

The question was why would the arrogant, go-for-the-throat Richard Winthrop Newton bet against his own horse? And did that have anything at all to do with his death?